Suddenly a 

he silence of th

Andrew lurched to his feet, threw open the bedroom door and saw the stranger on the bed, sobbing and crying.

"You're okay. You're okay," he soothed, and gathered her trembling body into his arms. Tears poured down her cheeks and she clung to him with the fierceness of a terrified child.

"You just had a bad dream," he said gently.

As her heartbeat seemed to slow, she stammered, "I'm—I'm sorry...."

"It's all right." He stroked her hair and lifted it away from her moist cheeks. "Everything will look different in the morning," he promised. He held her close until her breathing returned to normal, then eased her back down on the bed and left the room.

Sleep evaded him as he settled down for the night on the cot in the other room. Holding her in his arms had ignited some tender needs that he thought he'd buried a long time ago.

Turning restlessly on the narrow cot, Andrew tried to forget how soft and vulnerable she had felt in his arms.

Dear Harlequin Intrigue Reader,

We've got another month of sinister summer sizzlers lined up for you starting with the one and only Familiar—your favorite crime-solving black cat! Travel with the feisty feline on a magic carpet to the enchanting land of sheiks in Caroline Burnes's *Familiar Mirage*, the first part of FEAR FAMILIAR: DESERT MYSTERIES. You can look for the companion book, *Familiar Oasis*, next month.

Then it's back to the heart of the U.S.A. for another outstanding CONFIDENTIAL installment. This time, the sexiest undercover operatives around take on Chicago in this bestselling continuity series. Cassie Miles launches the whole shebang with *Not on His Watch*.

Debra Webb continues her COLBY AGENCY series with one more high-action, heart-pounding romantic suspense story in *Physical Evidence*. What these Colby agents won't do to solve a case—they'll even become prime suspects to take care of business...and fall in love.

Finally, esteemed Harlequin Intrigue author Leona Karr brings you a classic mystery about a woman who washes up on the shore sans memory. Good thing she's saved by a man determined to find her *Lost Identity*.

A great lineup to be sure. So make sure you pick up all four titles for the full Harlequin Intrigue reading experience.

Sincerely,

Denise O'Sullivan
Associate Senior Editor
Harlequin Intrigue

LOST IDENTITY

LEONA KARR

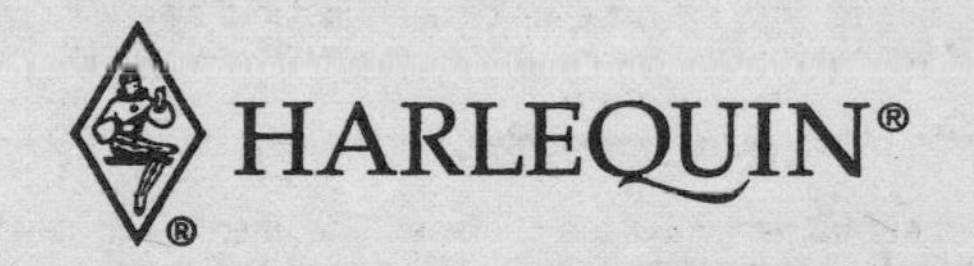

TORONTO • NEW YORK • LONDON
AMSTERDAM • PARIS • SYDNEY • HAMBURG
STOCKHOLM • ATHENS • TOKYO • MILAN • MADRID
PRAGUE • WARSAW • BUDAPEST • AUCKLAND

ISBN 0-373-22672-1

LOST IDENTITY

This edition published by arrangement with Harlequin Books S.A.

Visit us at www.eHarlequin.com

Printed in U.S.A.

ABOUT THE AUTHOR

A native of Colorado, Leona Karr lives at the foot of the Rocky Mountains with her husband, Michael. After pursuing a career as a reading specialist, she has followed her dream of becoming a writer, and is a multipublished author of romantic suspense, historicals, mysteries and inspirational romances. "Love conquers all" is the theme of her books, and she enjoys reading and writing fast-paced stories of danger and love.

Books by Leona Karr

HARLEQUIN INTRIGUE

120—TREASURE HUNT
144—FALCON'S CRY
184—HIDDEN SECRET
227—FLASHPOINT
262—CUPID'S DAGGER
309—BODYGUARD
366—THE CHARMER
459—FOLLOW ME HOME
487—MYSTERY DAD
574—INNOCENT WITNESS
623—THE MYSTERIOUS TWIN
672—LOST IDENTITY

Don't miss any of our special offers. Write to us at the following address for information on our newest releases.

Harlequin Reader Service
U.S.: 3010 Walden Ave., P.O. Box 1325, Buffalo, NY 14269
Canadian: P.O. Box 609, Fort Erie, Ont. L2A 5X3

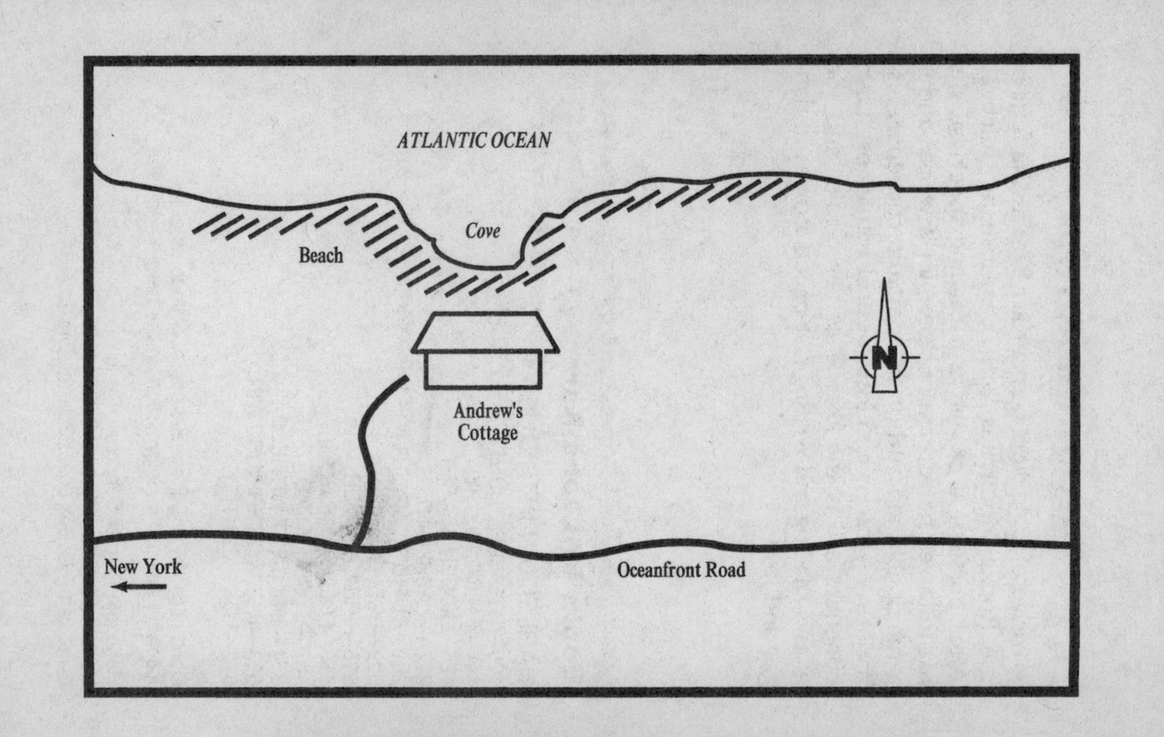
ATLANTIC OCEAN
Cove
Beach
Andrew's Cottage
N
New York
Oceanfront Road

CAST OF CHARACTERS

A mysterious young woman—She is nearly drowned on a deserted beach and has no memory of who she is or how she got there, but a terrifying sense of danger remains.

Andrew Davis—A solitary young man who offers his bungalow as a refuge. Will the discovery of the woman's identity change his life forever?

Perry Reynolds—A middle-aged successful business partner whose mysterious disappearance could be a hoax.

Curtis Mandel—A company executive who makes romantic claims that may be a clever cover-up.

Janelle Balfour—A friend and co-worker who has a familiarity with all that has happened in the past.

Darlene Reynolds—The angry young wife of Perry who has suspicions about her husband's disappearance.

Gary Reynolds—Perry's son. Is his need for money connected with his father's disappearance?

To my husband, Michael,
who fills my life with laughter, love and light.

Chapter One

Fierce winds and slashing rain whipped the New Jersey coastline as Andrew Davis stood at the window of his seaside cottage late one afternoon, and viewed the strong summer storm. Outside dark afternoon shadows mingled with curtains of slanting rain and thundering clouds. Warnings had been posted up and down the coast. He was about to draw the drapes when he glimpsed something unusual on the beach below. Even through the rivulets of rain pouring down the window glass, the shape of a human form lying on the sand was unmistakable.

Good Lord, could it be? A body washed up in the cove below his house?

Grabbing his slicker, he bounded out the door, took the deck stairs two at a time, and raced across the wild grass and sandy ground that lay between his elevated cottage and the beach below. When he reached the prone figure lying on the sand, he saw that it was a petite young woman lying on her back, her face stark white, framed by tangled dark hair drenched with seawater.

At his touch, she gave a weak groan, and then took in a gasp of air that told him her lungs were free of water. Her eyelids fluttered open and she gazed at him with rounded eyes filled with terror.

"It's all right," he assured her. "It's all right. Let's get you out of this storm." He scooped her up in his arms, and quickly carried her back to his cottage. Laying her down on a rug in front of the fire, he reached for a quilted cover to spread over her.

Her white slacks, soft pink blouse and white sandals were soaked. The clinging wet clothing defined the swell of her firm breasts, narrow waist and shapely legs. Her teeth were chattering, and her body was racked with shivers, but she seemed to be all right otherwise.

"I'll get you something warm to drink," he said and disappeared into his small kitchen.

She sat up, covered her face with hands and choked back a sob. A vertigo of unanswered questions swirled in her head, and fear was like a monster attacking her memory. Even as she struggled to fill the void in her mind, a deep terror shot through her. *Who is this man?* She couldn't remember anything beyond the moment when his anxious face bent over her. Even her very identity was lost in the dark abyss of her mind. *Was she afraid to remember?*

Andrew returned with a cup of coffee laced with brandy and said, "Here, this will warm you up."

Her blue lips murmured a weak, "Thank you."

He wasn't quite sure how to handle this unexpected houseguest. Should he suggest that she take a warm shower and put on some clothing of his? In her distraught condition, she might take offense. Obviously she had been traumatized by what had happened to her. How did she get on his beach? He'd been watching the storm develop all day, and hadn't seen any boats on this stretch of ocean. Weird, he thought.

He gave her a few moments to sip the drink, and then he said, "I'm Andrew Davis." When she didn't make the usual response, he waited for a long moment and then asked gently, "And your name is—?"

She lowered the cup, stared at it, and then said in a choked voice, "Trish." Even as she said it, there was no real familiarity with the name or any firm recognition that it belonged to her. Her stomach curled with tension. *Trish? Where did that name come from?*

"Should I call someone, Trish, and let them know that you're safe?"

Call who? A subtle warning lay somewhere in the devastating disorientation that she was experiencing. She lifted her head. "No, there's no one," she said as evenly as she could. *Why am I so frightened that someone will come for me?*

He raised an eyebrow, but didn't press her. She was obviously in a state of shock. Whatever had brought her to a deserted beach at the height of a lashing storm must have been catastrophic. Every time there was a clap of vibrating thunder, sparked by forks of summer lightning, she cringed as if she feared the fierce winds would whip the small cottage into the greedy ocean.

"This little house is storm-proof," he reassured her. "It's firmly anchored and has weathered gales a lot worse than this one." She nodded, but her sea-blue eyes remained glazed and rounded.

"Can I stay here...until...until the storm's over?" she asked, silently adding with a sense of helplessness, *until I remember where to go?*

"The welcome mat is always out for unexpected visitors," he lied. In truth, Andrew valued his privacy above everything else, and only an emergency like this one would compel him to share his roof with a stranger. "I'm curious how you found your way to my beach...well, not exactly mine," he admitted with a sheepish smile. "But I claim it."

She didn't respond, but the warmth of the fire and the stimulation of the hot drink began to ease her bone-deep chill. There was something reassuring about her rescuer's gentleness, his clean-cut looks, wavy blond hair bleached by the sun and his nicely tanned face. *I feel safe here,* she thought with a spurt of surprise. She stammered, "Maybe...maybe, I got lost."

"Lost?" Andrew waited for her to elaborate, but she didn't. What did she mean—maybe she got lost? Did she or didn't she? "You're not from around here, then?" he prodded.

Her hands tightened on her cup and she stared at it without answering.

Andrew decided to back off from any more questioning for the moment. He could tell that she was fighting for self-control, and whatever had happened to her had left her in a state of shock. No telling how long she would have to stay before the weather cleared and he could drive her somewhere. He decided that he'd have to take charge whether he wanted to or not.

"Would you like to take a hot shower, Trish, and get into some dry clothes? One of my long sweatshirts and bathrobes will keep you warm while we put your things through the washer and dryer."

She hesitated for a long moment and he could see uncertainty stamped on her face. Then she raised her head and nodded.

Like a child who is grateful for some adult direction, she followed him into the small bedroom.

Quickly, he laid out the clothes he'd mentioned, and then directed her to a small bathroom that adjoined his bedroom and the other small room, which he'd taken for his office.

"Here are some towels. Shampoo and soap are on the shelf. Make use of whatever is there, and if you need anything else, just holler."

After he had closed the door, she just stood there for a long moment, staring at herself in a mirror. Then she whispered, "Trish...Trish." Was that really the name of the strange woman with wide frightened blue eyes staring back at her? *What happened to me that I'm even afraid to remember who I am?* She shivered, and fought a weakness that went bone-deep.

She dropped her clothes, and searched her body for some familiar signs of recognition. There was an appendix scar, so she must have had it taken out at some time. Her toenails were polished in the same rosy hue as her fingernails. A bruise was forming on her right forearm and there was a tender spot on the back of her head. Had she fallen? Or had someone hit her? Had she suffered a blow to her head that had caused a momentary loss of memory? *Momentary.* She clung to that word as if it were a life preserver. Yes, she reassured herself, at any second, everything could come rushing back. Then she would know who she was, and why fear was coiled like a snake in the pit of her stomach.

AS ANDREW WAITED for her to join him again, this sudden intrusion into his contented and solitary life was creating some deep mixed feelings. Of course, he was glad that he'd been able to go to the woman's rescue, and would do it again in a minute, but at the same time, he sensed he was being drawn into something that was not to his liking.

As a developer of software for a major computer company, he worked at his beach cottage, and only commuted to the Manhattan office a couple of days a week. His life was ordered in a way that allowed almost complete privacy. He knew that his background as a foster child who had been constantly moved from one family to another had created this need to get away from the demands of other people. A couple of brief romantic relationships had not filled the empty void in his life, but had only resulted in more disappointments and a vow not to open himself up to that kind of pain again. He loved living alone, being accountable to no one, and having control over every aspect of his life. Just the sound of water running in his bathroom was a strange kind of intrusion. He wished that the storm would let up and he could drive the lady back to wherever she belonged.

Her vague answer about being lost was obviously a lie. *Was she running away from someone?* No sign of a wedding or engagement ring on her finger. He had noticed that her water-resistant watch was an expensive one, and her clothes certainly weren't bargain-basement. Who in the devil was she? And what was she doing on an isolated beach at the height of a storm?

When she came back into the living room a few minutes later, he was startled by the sudden change in her appearance. Her face was slightly pink from the warm shower, and fringed eyelashes and crescent eyebrows matched her clean, dark brown hair. There was a lift to her head that had not been there before, and he was strangely aware of a feminine loveliness about her that couldn't be disguised in his old plaid bathrobe, and faded argyle socks.

“I think I used up all your hot water,” she apologized, giving him a weak smile.

“No problem. It heats fast. You look much better.”

“I feel much better. Almost like myself.” *Whoever that might be,* she thought with a touch of painful irony.

“Good. I was about to put together some fish chowder for supper, would you like to join me in the kitchen and watch?” he asked, hoping she'd be more talkative if he maintained some kind of normalcy in the situation.

“Sounds good,” she said, pleased that she felt an honest reaction to his suggestion. Maybe she could rely on her gut feelings until she had something more tangible to give her insight. She followed him into the compact kitchen and sat down in one of the chairs beside a small round table.

As he reached into the refrigerator for the makings of his chowder, he asked. “Do you like to cook?”

She looked around the kitchen, her thoughtful eyes studied the counter canisters, spice rack and kitchen appliances. With a strange sense of certainty, she said firmly, “No, I don't. I'm not a good cook.”

Her expression puzzled him. Why did she look so pleased with herself? His suspicion that she was someone with money deepened. No doubt, she had hired help to do all the things that didn't appeal to her, like cooking.

“What do you like to do?” he asked, noticing her polished nails.

“Oh, lots of things,” she said vaguely, as muscles tightened around her mouth. She had no answer to the simple question, and she quickly turned away from it. "What about you?

He wasn't fooled. He had to admire the way she deftly avoided any talk about herself. Why was she so guarded about giving him any information? Was she running from the law? Could it be that he was harboring a fugitive? A spurt of resentment overtook him.

Ever since he'd purchased this cottage almost five years ago, he had jealously guarded his privacy. Even at the office, he was known as a loner, and although he was friendly enough with everyone, he avoided any personal intrusion in their lives, and he didn't invite any of them into his. He was thirty years old, and it was ironic that a strange woman sitting in his kitchen, wearing his robe, might be drawing him into some unwanted involvement that he had been careful to avoid.

As Andrew prepared the meal, he gave up trying to make any more conversation. Trish was aware of his withdrawal. Outside, the sounds of the relentless surf beating upon the beach below scraped her frayed nerves. Her safety seemed more tenuous than ever. She felt as if she were holding on to a lifeline that he'd thrown her, and would suddenly pull it away if she said the wrong thing.

What if she told him the truth? Would he believe her? Or would he think she was taking advantage of the situation and him? How could she describe the terror that swept up in her when she tried to remember? How could she explain the melodramatic truth that an ever-present danger lurked in the dark corners of her mind? She desperately needed to know the truth about who she was and what had happened to her before she opened herself up to anyone. An unknown terror reached out to her from the dark abyss of her lost memory.

Andrew sensed her inner turmoil as he served her a steaming bowl of chowder and corn bread muffins. "You'll feel better with some hot food in your stomach," he told her with a smile.

"It smells wonderful," she said, even as her tight stomach rebelled at the thought of food.

Instead of taking a chair opposite her at the tiny table, he perched on a high stool at a counter where he usually ate with a book in his hand. Her presence in the small kitchen seemed to demand some kind of social exchange, but her vague responses had discouraged any conversation between them.

She scarcely touched her food. "I'm sorry, I'm just not very hungry, after all," she apologized when he had finished eating his.

"That's okay. Sometimes food isn't the answer. You're probably needing a good night's sleep. I'll make up the cot in my computer room so you can have the bedroom."

"I don't want to inconvenience you like that," she protested, already sensing that just having her there was putting some kind of pressure on him.

"It's no bother," he answered politely. "Everything will look different in the morning."

"Yes, I'm sure it will." She forced a level of confidence into the words. Surely, whatever had caused her to lose her memory would be healed in sleep, allowing her to draw out of the depths of her unconscious the answers that were hidden from her. Somehow she knew that a temporary loss of memory could return as quickly as it was lost. Surely by morning she would know who she was, and why she had nearly lost her life in the raging storm.

ANDREW TRIED unsuccessfully to ignore the presence of the woman sleeping in his bed. As was his custom, he worked at his computer until after midnight, and then finally gave up because his mind kept wandering, plagued by unanswered questions about her. Why did he have a nagging suspicion that he was being used in some fashion? Even though his rescue of her seemed legit, could she have faked the whole thing for some nefarious purpose?

He plopped down on the living room couch. Sitting there and staring at the ebbing fire, he tried to come to some understanding of what he was feeling and what he should do next. His experience with conniving women had left him guarded and slightly bitter. He had long since decided that he wasn't cut out for the mating games that went with heavy dating. His few ventures into romantic relationships had proved what he already knew—opening oneself up only brought hurt, big time.

He leaned his head back on the couch and had just closed his eyes when a piercing scream rent the silence of the house. He lurched to his feet, threw open the bedroom door, and saw her writhing on the bed, sobbing and crying.

"You're okay. You're okay," he soothed and gathered her trembling body into his arms. Tears poured down her cheeks and she clung to him with the fierceness of a terrified child. Her breathing was rapid. Her body felt cold to his touch and she was caught in a spasm of shivers. Any doubts about her anguish being genuine were instantly dispelled. There was no way she could have pretended such an upheaval of emotion.

Trish heard his voice and struggled to find her way out of an enveloping panic. She clung to him and felt the warmth of his arms encircling her.

"You just had a bad dream," he said gently.

A bad dream. Her mind grabbed at his reassurance. *That's all it was. A nightmare.* Only fragments of images remained in her consciousness, and even as she tried to capture them, they faded away like shadows in a mist. Whatever had triggered the terror that had brought her screaming out of a tortured sleep, slipped away, leaving her empty and shaken.

As the drumming of her heart began to lessen, she managed to stammer, "I'm...I'm sorry..."

"It's all right." He stroked her hair and lifted it away from her moist cheeks, aware of the delicate contour of her face and the totally feminine body pressed against his. "Everything will look different in the morning," he promised once again. He held her close until her breathing settled into a normal rhythm, then he eased her back down on the bed and quietly left the room.

Sleep evaded him as he settled down for the night on the cot in his computer room. His mind kept turning over unanswered questions. He was certain now that she was truly frightened about something or someone. Although he was sympathetic to her situation, whatever it might be, he still didn't want to get involved. He suspected that there was a lover somewhere in the picture. She was very attractive, and more appealing than he was ready to admit. Holding her in his arms had ignited some tender needs that he thought he'd buried a long time ago. Turning restlessly on the narrow cot, he tried to forget how soft and vulnerable she had felt in his arms.

WHEN TRISH WOKE UP early the next morning, she was disoriented as she looked around the small room. Then a quiver of relief shot through her. She knew where she was. Everything came back from the moment that she'd been carried into the house. A man named Andrew had rescued her. And before that? And before that? The question kept ricocheting from one side of her head to the other.

Her lips quivered. Nothing. Nothing.

Hugging Andrew's faded robe around her, she walked to the window and stared at the scene stretched out before her. The summer storm had passed, leaving a soft mist moving away from the land.

Dragging her eyes over a small rocky cove below the cottage, she searched the empty beach and rolling breakers, struggling to recover some vision of what had happened to bring her to that deserted stretch of sand.

A new day lay fresh and glistening in the sunlight. She swallowed hard. A new day. For what? *Running and hiding? Running from what? Hiding from whom?* She turned back toward the bed, ready to crawl back in and cover up her head, but hesitated when she heard sounds in the other rooms.

Andrew was up. She knew he would be wanting some answers, but what should she tell him? If she admitted that she had no clue who she was, or how she had ended up on his beach, he would probably insist on taking her somewhere. Something deep within warned her not to leave this haven of safety until she could remember why she felt threatened and in danger. She decided to take the coward's way out—climb back in bed, cover up her head and pretend to be asleep.

Andrew prepared his usual breakfast of cereal and toast, and made two extra cups of coffee. This was one of his days in the office, but he'd hoped that he and his houseguest would have some time to talk before he left. Glancing at his watch, he knew that wasn't going to happen unless she got up in the next few minutes.

She didn't appear. The bedroom door was still closed when he was ready to leave. He listened for any sounds inside, and then quietly opened the door and peeked in. She was still in bed. He was about to close it again when she raised her head and gave him a startled look.

"Sorry, I didn't mean to wake you. I'm about to leave for the office." He frowned. He didn't feel right about leaving her after last night's sobbing nightmare, but he didn't have any choice. "Are you all right?"

"Yes," she readily lied. "Just tired."

"Well, sleep in as long as you like. I've left some breakfast for you." He hesitated, wanting to ask what her plans were, but it didn't seem to be the right time. After her ordeal yesterday and the kind of night she'd had, it was clear that she needed rest. He felt a little uneasy, leaving a stranger alone in his house, but he really had no choice. "I've left a note with my cell phone number if you want to call me."

She nodded.

There didn't seem to be anything more to be said so he closed the bedroom door and left the house. The whole business was unreal. Never in the world would he have imagined twenty-four hours ago that he would have a strange woman sleeping in his bed, sabotaging his well-ordered life and cluttering up his mind with irritating questions. As much as he hated to admit it, he couldn't forget the way she'd clung to him last night. He'd been careful not to allow anyone to be dependent upon him for anything, but there was something of a lost soul about her that could easily get to him if he let it. Anyway, she'd probably be gone when he got back home, he told himself, and he could chalk the whole episode up to some kind of weird adventure.

His unsettled mood must have been communicated to his fellow workers because several of them asked, "What's the matter with you today, Andrew? You don't seem like yourself."

He brushed off their comments with a shrug and vague answer. He couldn't help but laugh to himself, wondering what their reaction would be if he told them the truth—that there was a strange lovely waif sleeping in his bed.

As usual, Andrew had lunch by himself in the coffee shop that he frequented. He exchanged pleasantries with the motherly waitress who was used to serving him in a back booth where he ate his usual corned beef sandwich with a book opened on the table beside his plate. He tried to resume his usual routine, but when he found himself staring at the pages without reading the words, he pulled out his cell phone and called home.

No one answered.

He let it ring six times before he hung up. She must have left or was still sleeping. He didn't know whether he was relieved or irritated.

Later that afternoon, he called again. Still no answer.

TRISH HAD STAYED huddled in bed until midmorning. Finally, she took herself in hand, retrieved her clean clothes from the dryer and dressed. Thankful that she'd been given a slight reprieve from having to make any kind of decision, she went into the kitchen and poured herself a cup of coffee.

She saw that Andrew had left bread on the counter for toast and some cereal waiting to be heated on the stove, but her stomach was churning with too much anxiety to feel like eating anything.

What should she do? Where should she go?

Her mind played the questions over and over again. If she left the safety of this cottage, would she be walking straight into some unnamed danger? She knew with sickening certainty that something terrifying had happened to her, but that was all she knew. How could she protect herself when she didn't even know who she was or where the threat lay?

Taking the cup of hot coffee with her into the living room, she sat down in his easy chair. A faint masculine scent was strangely comforting as she thought about the man who had rescued her. Who was this Andrew Davis? His personal imprint was all over the small house. Wooden shelves flanking the fireplace were crowded with books of all kinds, and in the corner of the room was a guitar. Framed pictures on the wall were obviously prints taken with a simple camera, probably his, she thought. The modest furnishings suggested a man comfortable with himself, and a man who invited trust. She remembered how he had held her last night, and the way his gentle reassurances had soothed her shattered state. Up until now, he hadn't burdened her with a lot of questions, but she knew that that couldn't go on. She had to make a decision.

Either she was going to have to start lying or tell him the truth.

If she told him that she couldn't remember anything before he found her on the beach, would he believe her? He might think she was just trying to con him with such a tale, and show her the door. Where would she go?

Maybe a lie would be better, she reasoned. Almost any story would seem more acceptable than the truth. What kind of a tale could she weave that would make it reasonable for her to stay here until she had some glimmer of her lost identity?

The sudden ring of the telephone sent her into instant panic. She was afraid to answer. What if they asked, "Who is this?" And what was more frightening, someone might be trying to find her.

She held her breath until it stopped ringing. Too late, she realized that it might have been Andrew calling to see if she was still there. Maybe he had wanted to tell her that he expected her to be gone by the time he got home?

If only she could remember anything, even a glimmer, maybe she would know what to do. She hated the thought of going back down to the beach where he had found her, but maybe something there would trigger her memory. Nothing could be more terrifying than not knowing anything about what had happened to her.

Cautiously she opened the front door and peered out at a redwood deck that stretched across the front of the cottage on the ocean side. A small mahogany picnic table, benches and two matching chairs presented an inviting scene, but as she stood in the doorway, her feet refused to move outside. Her fear was stronger than her will.

Slamming the door shut, she leaned back against it with tears in her eyes and her fists clenched. Maybe she didn't know her name, but there was one question that was imbedded deep in every cell of her being.

Had she been fleeing for her life when Andrew found her on that beach?

Chapter Two

Andrew returned home that evening just after the sun had set. Twilight was slowly creeping across the ocean, and turning relentless rolling breakers into a dull gray. When he saw that there weren't any lights on in the cottage, he felt a momentary pang of disappointment. Although he was used to coming home to an empty house and grateful to be out of the hustle and bustle of the city, his mysterious houseguest had made this homecoming out of the ordinary. Just in case she might still be there, he had stopped and picked up some fried chicken and salad.

Well, so much for taking the time to plan supper, he thought, impatient with the whole situation. Even though he knew she'd been shaken by her ordeal, she could have had the courtesy to explain herself before she took off. She could have phoned him, he argued with himself, and then shoved the thought away. It didn't matter. Maybe it was better that she disappear as suddenly as she had come. At least she'd locked the door before she left, he thought as he let himself in.

As the door swung open, Trish jerked up from the

couch where she'd been lying, and her cry of terror was like a sharp knife renting the air.

"It's just me, Andrew," he said quickly as he flipped a light switch just inside the door.

"I thought...I thought..." She took a deep breath to steady her voice.

"I'm sorry I frightened you. The house was dark. I thought you'd gone, but I guess I woke you up?"

She wanted to run into his arms, let him hold her the way he had last night, and end the torturing long hours of trying to retrieve something that lay at the edges of her memory. His reassuring figure and concerned expression invited the kind of security that she desperately needed. Somehow, she knew she was safe now that he was home.

"Have you been sleeping all day?" he said, wondering why the telephone hadn't awakened her.

She nodded, not wanting to admit that for hours she'd been staring at the ceiling, trying to hold on to flickering impressions that faded too quickly for her to hold and examine them. Several times the darkness curtain in her mind seemed about ready to lift, causing her to hold her breathe as sweat beaded on her forehead. And then nothing.

"I brought supper," he said, holding up the sack that was redolent with the odor of fried chicken. "Did you raid the fridge and fix yourself some lunch?"

"I made some tea and nibbled on some cheese and crackers. I wasn't very hungry."

"Well, I'll fix us a couple of plates and we can go out on the deck to eat. The sun has burned off yesterday's rain, and it's going to be a lovely evening. Did you get out at all today?"

The question was casual, but it brought a tightness in her chest. "No, I stayed inside."

"I called a couple of times, but no one answered."

"I—I guess I must have been sleeping too hard to hear it."

He didn't believe her. The way she was avoiding his eyes spoke volumes. Why was she lying to him, and acting as if she was trying to come up with some believable story? He wanted to ask if she'd phoned anyone, or made arrangements to go back to wherever she belonged.

"Well, you probably needed the rest." She had touched a sympathetic chord in him, but loud and clear it vibrated with a warning. Her continued presence could completely upset his life. She'd already played havoc with his normal routine and he'd spent more time thinking about her than was wise.

"Why don't you freshen up, while I get things ready?" he suggested. After they had eaten, he'd insist that she level with him. He deserved to know what in the hell was going on.

She sensed his simmering impatience, and her stomach tightened as she went into the bathroom. Staring at herself, she was embarrassed at her disheveled appearance reflected in the mirror. Her hair was tangled, her eyes heavy, and deep lines of worry and fatigue etched her face. No wonder he had suggested that she freshen up. She was embarrassed that she'd let anyone see her in such a washed-out state. Somehow she knew that she'd always tried to look her best.

I have pride, she thought with a deep sense of satisfaction as she washed her face briskly with cold water. This little discovery was like a gem shining in a foggy darkness. It strengthened an inner confidence that seemed natural to her, and she glimpsed a tensile strength that had not been destroyed in the throes of amnesia.

I'll remember everything soon, she told herself as she carefully brushed her hair around the tender spot on the back of her head. She had just put the brush back on the shelf, and automatically reached out her hand to pick up something when she froze. Nothing was there.

For a split second the curtains of darkness in her head split and she could see a dark blue cosmetic bag decorated with bright butterflies just beyond her empty hand. The flash of remembrance was clear and unmistakable.

Joy like a surge of adrenaline shot through her. *I own a bright blue-and-yellow cosmetic bag. My memory is coming back!* Her heartbeat quickened and the palms of her hands were suddenly moist with sweat. It wasn't much, but it was a beginning.

With a stronger step, she hurried out to the living room to join Andrew, but he was already outside on the deck. She saw him through the large picture window. He had lit some patio lamps, which sent a soft glow over the deck.

"Come on out. Food's ready." Andrew gave her an inviting wave of his hand.

As Trish stood in the doorway, looking out, her burst of well-being faded. Her mouth went dry and her chest was suddenly weighted. She fixed her eyes on Andrew's reassuring figure as she slowly pushed opened the screen, and forced herself to step out on the deck.

As her frantic gaze searched the beach below the house, she didn't know what or whom she was expecting to see. In the twilight only a peaceful scene of water, sand and sky greeted her eyes. She saw that Andrew's house was nestled in a small cove isolated from other structures whose roofs she could glimpse in both directions some distance away.

Andrew was puzzled by the visible signs of a struggle going on inside her as she stood there, her eyes searching in every direction. Had she expected to see something or someone? She was certainly attractive enough to have a man chasing after her. Had she been fleeing from a lovers' quarrel when she got lost in the storm? By this time, the poor guy was probably frantic from her disappearance.

Andrew suddenly had a bad taste in his mouth. This kind of speculation didn't sit well with him. Her reluctance to go back and face the situation gave him the feeling that she was just using him.

He said rather stiffly, "Have a seat. I'm sorry it isn't more. I'm afraid my bachelor life is lacking in the finer things of life."

She shot him a quick look as she sat down on the bench facing him. He'd never used that tone with her before, and she knew what was coming. She had overstayed her welcome. Her stomach tightened. If only he would give her a little more time to remember why she had a deep fear of someone knowing where she was. Any story she'd been able to think of had too many holes in it to convince him to let her stay. If she lied about being on vacation alone, her belongings would have to be somewhere. No doubt, he would offer to drive her back to her lodgings, and then what?

Sitting across the table from her, Andrew watched her pick at her chicken and salad, really not eating but just going through the motions. Was she putting on an act? He'd been taken in by manipulating women when he first came to the city, but he'd learned his lesson. Hadn't he? Looking at her appealing femininity, he wasn't sure.

He set down the chicken leg he'd been eating, wiped his hands and then leaned toward her. "I think it's time you leveled with me, Trish, don't you?"

She deliberately took a drink of water, delaying the moment when she'd have to speak. She wished now that she'd told him the truth in the beginning, but she'd been too frightened to think clearly. Like a hunted animal, a deep protective instinct had warned to protect herself.

"All right. Let me guess," he said when she was slow in answering. "You're running away from some unpleasant situation that you don't want to face."

"Maybe." *I don't know. I don't know.*

"Maybe?" he repeated, with a disbelieving edge to his voice. "Either you are or you aren't, Trish. Frankly, I suspect that some man is beside himself wondering where you are."

"Do you think so?" she asked almost in a whisper.

The anguish that flashed across her face made him soften his tone even though he was getting impatient with her evasiveness. "Trish, I'm thankful that I was around when you needed rescuing, but hiding out here isn't going to work for you—or for me, either."

"I know." She sighed. "You've been more than patient, and I don't know what I would have done if...if you hadn't found me."

"You've got to face up to whomever, or whatever you're running away from, Trish." He reached across the table and took her hand. "Why don't you tell me about what was going on?"

She laced her fingers through his, drawing strength from the contact. Maybe he would accept the truth. Or would he just think she was making everything up in an effort to wring enough sympathy from him so he'd let her stay?

"What is it, Trish? I have to know."

She drew in a deep breath to settle the quivering in her chest. "The truth is that I don't know who I am. And I need a little time to figure it out."

His mouth quirked as if he didn't know whether to laugh or let his irritation show. "That's the metaphysical question for this generation, isn't it? Who am I? I can't believe how many people get on this quest—"

"That isn't what I mean." She jerked her hand away from his. Her eyes flashed as she said each word with loud emphasis, "Don't you understand? I don't know who I am."

Andrew simply stared at her.

"I've lost my memory. I remember your rescuing me from the beach. But that's all. Nothing before that."

"I see." An inner voice warned him to be careful. "You have amnesia." Skepticism laced the statement.

Trish could tell from his tone that he didn't believe her. He obviously thought she was trying to put something over on him. Her hopes that he would understand took a sickening dive. Any lie she could have dreamed up would have had a better response from him than the truth.

"Yes, I have amnesia," she repeated firmly.

"Well, that is a problem, isn't it?" he said as if he were addressing a child who had just told a whopper of a lie.

''Don't patronize me,'' she flared. ''I'm telling you the truth. I don't remember anything from the moment I opened my eyes and saw your face bending over me.''

''But you said your name was Trish,'' he protested. ''Did you just make that up?''

She hesitated, and then answered thoughtfully, ''I don't think so. The name just kind of floated up and seemed familiar.''

''And you don't remember anything else?''

''I know I have a blue-and-yellow cosmetic bag with butterflies on it. I remember that,'' she said triumphantly.

He watched as her blue-green eyes lost their flatness. There was such joyful thankfulness in her face when she said she had remembered the bag that he had a hard time believing it was just an act. Still, it was a stretch to accept this bizarre story as the truth.

''You don't believe me, do you?'' She sighed, watching his brown eyes narrow as he looked at her, and deep lines furrow his forehead.

''Frankly, I don't know whether I do or not,'' he answered honestly. He'd heard of retrograde amnesia when a person would remember things after a trauma and nothing before. Clearly she'd been in a state of shock when he'd found her on the beach, but keeping such a frightening state to herself didn't seem rational. Was this very appealing woman cleverly manipulating him to her own ends?

''I'm telling you the truth,'' she insisted, reading the skepticism in his expression.

''You have to admit that you've been rather adept at keeping your loss of memory from me. I mean, I would have thought you would have told me right away.''

''I couldn't.''

''Why not?''

''Because...because I had to protect myself any way I could.'' Her gaze dragged his face with pleading intensity. ''Deep down I knew that I was being threatened by something or someone. By keeping quiet, I was just trying to protect myself—and you—until I could remember and know what to do.''

Andrew's thoughts whirled like dry leaves caught in a devil's wind. He knew that her nightmare had been real enough. Some of her vague answers and behavior could be symptoms of complete disorientation. When he thought about her behavior in the context of her not remembering anything, there was a ring of authenticity about it. Still, her determination to keep such an appalling state a secret bothered him. ''You should have told me.''

''I know. I'm sorry.''

''How long did you plan to keep me in the dark?''

''I thought—I hoped—that at any moment, my memory would come back. Plus I wasn't sure you'd believe me if I told you the truth.''

He hesitated. ''I've heard about people losing their memory when something horrendous happens to them.''

Her lips quivered as she looked across the table at him. ''I don't know why I'm in danger, but it's a deep-gut feeling that I can't deny. I feel safe here with you, Andrew, and that's why I don't want to leave. Please say that I can stay.''

All rational arguments against opening himself up to this disruptive intrusion in his life fled. He walked around the table and eased down beside her. Putting an arm around her slumped shoulders, he heard himself saying, ''Of course, you can stay. We'll sort this thing out.''

He felt a surge of protectiveness that was alien to anything he'd felt before. His cautious, rational approach to life deserted him as he was suddenly filled with desires that made him a stranger to a surge of bewildering hunger. He wanted to trace the sweet curve of her cheeks with his fingertips, and bury his lips in the smooth loveliness of her neck. He bent his head close to hers and as a soft breeze tugged at wayward strands framing her face, he knew that in another moment, he would forget himself completely.

Gently he withdrew his arm and took a steadying breath, hoping that she was unaware of his physical response to her nearness.

''There are things that we can do right away to find some of the answers,'' he said, allowing his methodical intellectual nature to take over. Then he added as lightly as he could, ''We'll find out why you showed up like a drowned kitten on my doorstep, and it will all make sense. Until then try to relax, and let me see what I can find out. Okay?''

Gratitude made her voice unsteady as she thanked him. ''I'll try not to be an intrusion. Why don't you let me sleep on the cot?''

''No, I like to work late, and sometimes get up in the middle of the night to try out an idea. It's better if you take the bedroom.'' He eyed her nearly untouched plate. ''I guess you don't like chicken.''

''Yes, I do.'' She found herself relaxing for the first time since her rescue. ''It's strange, but I seem to know things like that—what I like and what I don't like. I saw your guitar in the house and I know I like music but I'm not sure what kind. Some of the books on your shelves seemed familiar even though I can't actually remember reading them.'' She frowned. ''That's weird, isn't it? I know a lot about myself, but none of the important things like what my name is and why I have a compelling instinct to hide.'' She shivered. ''None of it makes sense, does it?''

''It will make sense when we know the whole story.''

A sudden tightening in her chest made her plead, ''But don't let anyone know I'm here, not until we know for sure who I am. Promise?''

''Promise.''

Even though his mind had already been racing ahead to printing flyers with her picture on it, he knew she was right. If she had been a victim of foul play, it wouldn't be wise to let other people know who and where she was until they found out the whole story.

''What do you think we should do first?'' she asked, her spirits rising with hope for the first time.

''I'll get a list of missing people in the area, and you can look over the names and see if any of them seem slightly familiar. We'll go from there.''

His confidence was like a healing balm and when they went back inside the house, Trish felt stronger and less fearful than she had before, and she chided herself for not telling him sooner. She was able to look at her situation in a rational light for the first time. She belonged somewhere. She had connections to others. Every question in her dark memory had an answer.

''Getting impatient isn't going to help,'' Andrew had warned her earlier when she confided in him that not knowing the simplest things about herself was devastating.

She knew that he had been skeptical in the beginning, and who could blame him? This whole scenario was something out of a soap opera. But in the end, he had believed her. The warmth of his protective arm around her spoke volumes. She had an ally. She was no longer alone.

THAT NIGHT, ANDREW USED his computer to run off everything he could find on amnesia due to traumatic shock. When it came to facing any problem, he was always meticulous in his approach. That was just his nature, and one of things that made him successful in creating sophisticated software. By the time he turned off the computer, he had a fistful of research material.

He quietly went back into the living room and slumped down in his easy chair as he studied the printouts. The mantel clock was striking two o'clock when he finished reading.

Experts seemed to agree that hysterical amnesia resulted from a person's desire to dissociate from a particularly intolerable situation when the victim chose to block out that incident and everything that went before it.

Leaning his head against the back of the chair, he closed his eyes as he tried to digest the information. One unrelenting question stabbed at him with demanding clarity.

What was the intolerable situation that made Trish choose to lose her memory?

Chapter Three

When Trish got up the next morning, Andrew was already gone, and her sense of well-being faded instantly as she faced another long day alone. Somehow she hadn't expected him to go to the office two days in a row. Even though she was tempted to go back to bed, she dressed slowly in the undergarments she'd washed out the night before, and put on the same white slacks and blouse.

The same swirl of disorientation poured over her as she moved about the kitchen. Just like the first morning, he had made coffee, but there was no sign that he'd already had breakfast. Maybe he hadn't gone to work. Her hands were suddenly clammy and cold even though they circled a hot mug. Could he have decided to take matters into his own hands and gone to the authorities? What if he reported that a strange, delusional woman had invaded his house? Surely, the authorities would come for her. And then what? Maybe she was responsible for something terrible. For the first time, she entertained an unnamed guilt, and a fear that whatever had happened to her, she had brought it on herself.

Panic suddenly overwhelmed her. She set down her

coffee cup with such force that the liquid spilled all over the table. Everything that lay hidden in her mind seemed to crystallize in one thought—she had to leave the house before the danger lurking in the shadows of her memory found her.

She lurched up from her chair and started across the kitchen toward the back door, but before she reached it, she stopped dead in her tracks, frozen in horror. She was too late! The firm sound of footsteps warned her that someone was coming up the back stairs. They were already here! Before she could turn on her heels and flee, the door opened and she screamed.

Andrew stared at her in disbelief. "Trish, for godsake, what's the matter?" He'd never seen raw terror on anyone's face before, but he saw it on hers.

"Andrew," she breathed, giddy with relief.

"You look as if you were expecting a ghost." He was wearing a jogging suit, running shoes, and his moist sun-streaked hair was held back with a sweatband.

"Not a ghost," she managed, leaning up against the counter to keep her weak knees from buckling.

He searched her ashen face. Who had she expected to see coming through the door? Had her memory returned? "Tell me what's going on, Trish. I'm not used to being greeted with bone-chilling screams when I come in the door—at least, not so early in the morning," he added, trying to lighten the situation.

She ran an agitated hand through her dark hair. "I guess I let my imagination run away with me," she admitted, totally embarrassed by the way she had lost control. "I'm sorry. When you weren't here, I thought you'd decided to turn me over to someone else. And that frightened me."

Even though he knew that in her present state, she was vulnerable to distrust, it really bothered him that she thought him capable of callously tossing her out of his house. "I thought we'd agreed on how we were going to handle this thing? Didn't we?"

His briskness told her that she had offended him, but she didn't know how to explain that the frightening scenario had developed in her mind because of his absence. She nodded, not wanting to admit that panic had driven everything out of her mind.

"All right, then." His tone softened. "I promise I won't do anything without your approval."

"I'm sorry I jumped to conclusions."

"You should be. I don't recall that anything was said about me bringing a paddy wagon up to the back door and hauling you away," he chided. "At least, not before breakfast."

In his teasing smile, she saw a steady uncompromising strength that invited her to trust him. She prayed that whatever truth she discovered about herself would not destroy that trust.

"Now, sit down and finish your coffee while I whip up some French toast. *Oui, Mademoiselle?*"

She laughed at his corny accent, and couldn't believe how deftly he had changed the whole timber of the day. For the first time since her rescue, her past didn't seem as important as letting herself momentarily enjoy the present moment.

As the day progressed, there were times when she wished that he wasn't so intent upon following up every avenue that might end the protective sanctuary that she'd found with him. Deep down, she knew that she was using him as an anchor in the morass of her unknown problems, and that it wasn't fair to attach herself to him on any emotional level, but she couldn't help herself.

When he brought her a list of the people who had been reported lost in the state of New Jersey since the storm, she carefully read every name of women in her age group. Saying the name aloud, she paused to see if there was any flicker of familiarity. When she'd made it through the list, her lips trembled as she handed it back to him.

"If my name is there, I don't recognize it."

"It's okay. There are other lists," he reassured her, even as he hoped that they wouldn't have to go through the missing persons records for every state in the union. She could have come to New Jersey from anywhere and for a thousand different reasons. "I'll get a similar list from New York City and Long Island."

When he gave them to her, Trish was appalled at the hundreds of names of people reported missing in only a three-day period. Once again, she tried to connect any kind of memory with each of the possible names, but with the same result.

"Nothing. I guess this isn't going to work," she said, holding back a wash of despair.

He was silent for a moment. "Of course, the best way to handle this might be to come at it from a different way," he said thoughtfully. "We could pass out flyers with your description and picture and see if—"

"No!" she protested vehemently. "I have to know who I am first. Don't you understand?"

"I'm not sure I do," he said quietly. She was suddenly like a wild creature backed into a corner. "I would think that you'd want to use any means you could to find out who you are."

She searched for words that would help him understand. Drawing a shaky breath, she tried to explain. "There is some deep terror buried within me. I don't know how to explain it, but I'm afraid that whatever happened to me before is out there waiting to happen again. I have to find out who I am before I'll feel safe."

"You think someone is waiting to do you harm?"

"I don't know what I think. I just *know* that I don't want to put out my picture all over the place. Not yet. Not until I have a chance to discover my identity." She sighed. "I don't know, maybe I'm just paranoid because I can't remember what happened to me."

"I don't think paranoid is a characteristic of amnesia," he admitted. "There must be something more there, and I don't think we should do anything that doesn't sit well with you. At least for the time beginning, let's concentrate on coaxing your memory back. Okay?"

She gave him a relieved smile. "What do you suggest we do next?"

"How about a walk down to the beach?" he suggested casually as if it was just a pleasant idea. He watched myriad emotions cross her face as fright, refusal and then determination gave way to a stubborn lift of her chin.

"All right. I suppose that's a good place to start."

He admired the way she was fighting the demons in her mind. "If things get too tense for you, just say so, and we'll leave it for another day."

As they stepped out on the deck, Trish felt a rush of adrenaline that was like a charged current surging through her. She stiffened her resolve not to be defeated by emotions warring within her. If she could just make it down to the place where Andrew had found her, everything might come rushing back. Maybe the blocks in her mind would fall away and she would see what was hidden from her. She swallowed back her fear and stiffened her resolve to accept anything that her memory threw back at her. Anything.

"You, okay?" he asked as she stiffly walked beside him. When he reached out and took her hand, he was surprised how clammy it felt. She looked like someone walking to her execution. With a start, he realized the strength of will she was displaying in leaving the house and exposing herself to whatever upheaval might be waiting for her. "It's going to be all right. Don't be frightened."

"I'm not," she lied.

He tried to get her mind off the purpose for their walk. "It's a beautiful view, isn't it?"

"Yes," she said without looking at it.

"Why don't we take a little walk in the other direction before we circle the cove?"

She hesitated for a moment, and then nodded. The reprieve, even for a few moments, was a welcome blessing.

They crossed a wide strip of sandy ground dotted with wild grass, sand, rocks and driftwood, and carefully made their way down to the beach. As they walked along the edge of the water, seagulls darted overhead, keeping up a cacophony of raucous noise. The ocean simmered in the bright light of the sun, and a light breeze ruffled the water, sending a frill of white dancing to the shore.

Trying to ease her nervousness, Andrew talked a little bit about the coastline and the terrain farther south. Nothing he said about the geography seemed to register with her, but her body lost some of its tension as she walked beside him. Her hand felt small and fragile in his, and glancing at her profile, he realized again how petite and feminine she was. It was beyond his comprehension why anyone would want to hurt her. Was her trauma centered on her loss of memory and nothing more?

She felt his searching gaze upon her, and she gave him a tenuous smile. With his strong body so close to hers, she felt safely anchored in the moment. When he smiled back at her, his brown eyes catching a glint of sunlight in their depths, she felt a strange stirring that unwittingly brought warmth into her cheeks.

They walked for about a half mile before they turned back, and he felt her tension returning as they neared the cove that lay below his cottage. The sandy beach narrowed at this point. In this small scallop of the coastline, dry seaweed and bleached driftwood lay among rocks that edged small eddies. A couple of indignant gulls rose with a flutter of wings from one of the small pools.

"Let's see now," he said in a conversational tone. "If I remember right, you were lying just about there."

She stopped and looked down at the smooth sand as if the indentation of her body should still be there. "Are you sure?"

He glanced up at his house. "Yes, I could see this spot through the front window."

She moistened her dry lips. "Did you see anybody else? Or anything?"

"Nope. I just glimpsed you lying right here. No sign of a boat or anything else."

"Then how did I get here?" she asked, frowning, as if he were somehow keeping the answer from her.

"That's what we need to figure out."

She had steeled herself to accept whatever her mind dredged up, and she felt like someone ready to do battle without any enemy to fight. How could they find any answers when her memory was as blank as a freshly washed surface?

"Why don't we sit down, and just take it easy for a few minutes? You can look around and once you get oriented, you may remember something."

"And what if I don't?"

"Then I guess we're back to square one," he said, not wanting to admit he'd put a lot of hope in her remembering something that would give them a place to start. He was convinced that if they didn't have some kind of a breakthrough, there was no other alternative but to get her some professional help. Without even suggesting such an idea, he knew what her response would be.

She sat on the sand, hugged her pulled-up legs with her arms, and resisted the temptation to bury her face against her knees. Biting her lower lip, she looked out at the waves breaking in white-foamed sprays against rocks outlining the inlet. She narrowed her eyes, trying to superimpose another scene upon one in her view, but she failed. Nothing in the way of a memory came to her. She only knew that the sound of roaring surf was one that had tortured her and brought cold chills rippling down her spine.

Sitting close beside her, Andrew watched her face and sensed the struggle going on within her. "Just try to relax, Trish, and let your mind wander where it will.

Forcing yourself to remember will only make you more tense.''

They sat in a heavy silence for several long minutes, until Trish couldn't take it any longer. She turned to him. ''Talk to me. About anything.''

''All right. See that tern pecking away over there?'' he pointed to a small white bird hopping about as if she were riding a pogo stick. His resonant voice softened. ''She's got a nest over there in the rushes, and in the early spring there were five little ones following her around. They've all gone now, seeking their fortune in the big wide world.'' He described other water fowl that were frequent visitors to the small cove as if they were his friends and companions.

Just listening to his steady unruffled voice was strangely soothing. She stretched her legs out in front of her and leaned back on her arms, pretending that there was nothing more urgent than just listening to him.

''I collect a lot of driftwood in this spot. For some reason the current seems to swing into this small cove. I suppose that anything or anyone caught in the surf might end up here.'' He watched for any slight flicker of her eyelids but her expression remained impassive.

She knew what he was trying to do—prime her memory pump. But it didn't work. All she could remember was lying in that very spot, gasping for air, not knowing if her clothes were drenched either from seawater or the pouring rain.

''Where do you go on your morning run?'' she asked, wanting to get his attention on something else besides her complete lack of success in remembering anything before he found her.

''Sometimes I make it down the coast to those

buildings whose roofs you can see,'' he said as he pointed southward. ''A little over a mile. There's a small shopping center and a couple of resort hotels. Just a nice walk from here—in nice weather.''

Getting to her feet, she stared in the direction he had been pointing. ''Do you think I could have walked in the storm from there to here?''

''Do you?'' he asked quietly.

''It's possible, isn't it?'' Nervous hope suddenly churned her stomach. ''Maybe I was stupid enough to hike this far in the rainstorm and was overcome by fatigue. That could be it, couldn't it?''

''What do you say to getting in the car and taking a quick look around Seaside Plaza? We can see if anything rings a bell,'' Andrew suggested as he rose to his feet. ''You don't have to get out of the car unless you want to.''

Instant refusal caught in her throat. Leaving the safety of Andrew's cottage was the last thing she wanted to do.

''Come on, let's give it a try,'' he coaxed as he slipped an arm around her waist and guided her back to the house.

In a matter of minutes, she found herself crowded close beside him in the front seat of his small car, her chest tight and her breathing rapid. Something deep within her didn't accept the explanation that her present condition was the result of something as benign as a misguided walk.

Aware of her intense physical reaction, Andrew began to wonder if it was such a good idea after all to make her leave the house. She looked almost physically ill hunched down in her seat. He was tempted to turn the car around and go back to the cottage, but he knew that sooner or later, she would have to get out in public. The possibility that they might find some inkling of her identity so close to his place stiffened his resolve to see the thing through.

A fashionable resort hotel had been built on the beach in the center of a landscaped square bordered by inviting tourist shops. Driving slowly past the hotel, Andrew gave her a chance to look at the front of the building. Through large front glass windows and doors, they could catch glimpses of the elegant interior. He reasoned that if Trish had been staying at the hotel, she would be familiar with it and the surrounding stores.

Just as they passed the front entrance, two men and a woman came out the front door of the hotel, and instantly Trish hunched down in the seat.

''Do you think you know them?'' Andrew asked quickly. ''Do they look familiar?''

She shook her head. Nothing looked familiar. Not the hotel. And her driving instinct was to hide from any stranger. How could she make him understand that this total lack of recognition was the reason enough to hide from an unnamed terror that kept her from remembering?

''How about any of the shops? Any of them ring a bell?'' He asked as he parked the car so she could view the front of the various stores.

After a moment of letting her searching gaze rove around the busy plaza, she reluctantly shook her head. Sitting there in her one set of clothes, there were dozens of things in the colorful window displays that she wished she could walk in and buy, but none of the store names or fronts registered any recognition. If she had shopped there, she didn't remember anything about it.''

''Well, just relax and be a people-watcher for a few minutes. I'll be back right back.'' He opened his door and slipped out of the car.

Before she could protest, he had taken off with a leisurely stride and headed down the walk toward the hotel. She didn't know whether to yell at him to come back, or go after him. In the end, she did neither.

''It's all right,'' she told herself, taking some deep breaths to center herself. She had to trust him. There was no reason to believe that he was going to abandon her. She leaned her head back on the seat and closed her eyes. She knew that the fatigue that swept over her body was born of a fear of betrayal.

Betrayal. The way the word shot through her, startled her. She sat up with a jerk. A flash of betrayal triggered a series of vague images that slithered by too fast for her to grab them. A sudden, slight lifting of the shadows in her mind caught her off guard. A memory was almost there, but it lacked form. It was like waking up from a dream, and not quite remembering. Only the emotion remained. She felt weak and shaken, and yet, strangely elated. *She had been betrayed. She knew it!*

When Andrew returned to the car a few minutes later, he was startled by the change in her posture and expression. Her earlier glazed, dull expression was gone. Her face was animated and her blue eyes were shining.

''What happened? Did you remember something?''

''Almost,'' she said, smiling. ''I almost remembered something.''

''Almost?'' He had been ready for her to declare

that she remembered who she was. His elation faded slightly as he asked, "What happened?"

"I saw some images. Just for a few seconds," she explained. "They flickered past too vague and quickly for me to examine them." She saw disappointment tug at the corner of his lips so she grabbed his hand. "Next time I might be able to hold on to them long enough to really recognize and remember them. It's a start—don't you see?"

Her excitement was contagious. Her sudden animation took him by surprise. For the first time, he caught a glimpse of a vivacious, confident woman who would not be defeated by the devastating shock she had suffered.

"Yes, it's a start," he agreed, smiling even though he didn't know exactly what she was talking about. Had she wanted to remember something so badly that her mind was playing tricks on her? "Do you know what triggered these images?"

"Not really. I was just sitting here wondering if you had abandoned me." She shot him an apologetic look. "The feeling of betrayal seemed to take over for a few seconds and that's when it happened."

"I really don't know what to say, Trish." He squeezed the hand still locked in his. "Let's give it some thought, and see what we should do next. I checked at the hotel, pretending to be a reporter doing an article on the storm. I asked if all their guests were accounted for, and they assured me that they were, but, of course, there's no way of knowing if you were registered—unless we show them a picture."

"No," she said firmly, withdrawing her hand. *You don't give your enemies an advantage.* She didn't realize she'd said it aloud until she saw his startled expression.

"If you really believe that, Trish," he said firmly, "then it's time to get you some professional help. What happened today might be a breakthrough if you had the right kind of counseling."

"You mean psychiatric care?" she flared. "Just because I can't remember, doesn't mean I should be committed to some booby hatch." Even as she heard herself, she knew she was like a child throwing a tantrum because she didn't want to go to the doctor.

"I'm sure we can find a respectable clinic that can provide the kind of help you need," he said in a quiet, reassuring way. "Just think about it."

She fell silent as he drove back to the cottage. Even though she desperately wanted a breakthrough as quickly as possible, the idea of putting herself in the hands of perfect strangers was terrifying. She wasn't even sure that she could depend on Andrew to remain as her main anchor. Maybe he was urging her to seek help because he didn't want to be involved with her any further.

When they got back to the house, he suggested that she take a nap while he caught up on some work. As soon as she was settled in the bedroom, he left his computer and took his cell phone out on the deck. One of his female co-workers had spent some time at a small mental health hospital after a nervous breakdown, and she'd only had positive things to say about the care she'd been given. He made a quick call to her and she gladly gave him the number he needed.

Andrew phoned the hospital, and asked to speak to one of the resident doctors concerning the admittance of an amnesia patient. He was referred to a Dr. Jon

Duboise. As succinctly as Andrew could, he explained to the doctor about Trish's condition.

"She has a deep fear that someone will find her before she can remember what happened to her. Whatever it was must have been something traumatic."

"Reason enough for her to block out the memory," the doctor agreed. "The loss of memory about an emotionally traumatic event is usually the result of a person's desire to dissociate from a particularly intolerable situation."

"And once she's willing to recall that event, will she get her memory back?" Andrew asked hopefully.

"If it's hysterical or post-traumatic retrograde amnesia, it's very likely," Duboise explained. "But even with therapy, it could take time." He asked a few more questions, and then assured Andrew that privacy was a top priority at Havengate Hospital.

Andrew thanked him and hung up without committing himself to anything. He sat out on the deck for several minutes trying to come up with the best way to handle Trish. Her aversion to exposing herself to anyone was clear. He knew that she would accuse him of withdrawing his support if he insisted that she check herself into a hospital. She had already admitted that she feared his betrayal.

He decided to wait until evening before saying anything. When she emerged from the bedroom, he noted that she had, undoubtedly, taken his advice and had a long nap. She was more rested than he'd seen her. At dinner, she even ate a nice helping of his spaghetti and meatballs.

They had coffee in the living room, and impulsively he picked up his guitar and began strumming some familiar tunes. Trish curled up on the couch, smiling as she watched his dexterous fingers find the chords with an easy pleasure. She could tell that he was used to spending evenings in the company of his guitar. A soft wave of blond hair drifted forward as he bent his head over the instrument. Her eyes followed the strong sweep of his cheeks and jaw, and lingered on the fullness of his mouth. She greedily captured every detail in her mind, knowing that she would draw on this memory over and over again, no matter how many others were denied her. She felt a peculiar stirring inside that made her want to shut out the rest of the world and hold on to this sweet moment forever. At that moment, she realized she was dangerously close to allowing her feelings to deepen for this blond-headed troubadour.

Andrew was pleased with the soft smile on her face and he was glad he'd broken his rule never to play for anyone but himself. None of his co-workers at the office even suspected he knew one note from another, and as Trish began humming some of the tunes, he experienced sudden companionship that had been rare in his life.

He gave her an encouraging grin as very softly she began singing along with his playing, as though testing her memory for the words. She had a lovely clear voice, and her confidence grew. When he began strumming a bouncy tune, she started clapping in rhythm, and he glimpsed an outgoing, perky manner that he hadn't seen before. He ended the song with a flourish of chords that left them both laughing.

"Hey, you're good." He grinned at her as he set aside his guitar.

"I love to sing," she admitted with wide-eyed surprise. Knowing one more thing about herself was like finding another piece of a hidden puzzle.

"We make a good team. Shall we go on the road?"

"I wish we could," she answered wistfully as a cloud descended on her face, erasing the brightness that had been in her eyes only moments before.

Andrew realized immediately that he'd said the wrong thing. Even in jest, talking about the future was painful for her. He eased down beside her on the couch. Maybe the time had come to tell her about the call he'd made to Havengate Hospital.

"Trish, there's something we need to talk about."

Instantly her sense of well-being took a dive. *Here it comes,* she thought. *He's going to tell me it's time to move on.* He put his arm around her shoulder, but she sat stiffly beside him.

"All right, let's talk," she said as steadily as the quivering in her stomach would allow.

"I talked with a Dr. Duboise about you and—"

"What? You didn't!" Her voice was strident. "You promised!"

"I said that I wouldn't do anything to jeopardize your safety, and I didn't." He kept his tone even and controlled. "Let me explain."

"I trusted you," she lashed out, and started to get up, but he pulled her back down.

"Just listen, please." Putting his hands firmly on her shoulders, he looked directly into her rounded eyes. He could see the wild pulse beating in her neck. "There's a Havengate Hospital near here, and they treat amnesia patients. You need professional help, Trish."

"And you want me out of your hair," she flared angrily and tried to push him away.

"Trish, you can't do this on your own."

"If you'd just give me a little time," she pleaded. "After all, it's only been three days."

"And what if it becomes three months? What then? Are you willing to suffer not knowing who you are, and what happened to drive away your memory for months and perhaps even years?" He softened his voice. "You're a beautiful young woman, and you deserve better than that."

"But what if someone finds me before...before my memory comes back?" She swallowed hard, feeling as if she'd suddenly been swept up in a whirlwind over which she had no control.

"Dr. Duboise has promised complete secrecy about your presence there."

"But what about payment? They'll admit me to a place like that out of the goodness of their hearts?"

"Almost," he admitted with a reassuring smile. He could tell that her initial defensiveness was easing, and he dropped his hands from her shoulder. "Havengate is supported by a philanthropic trust fund. The hospital will accept you without payment with the belief that after you recover your identity, you'll be able to settle with them financially. According to Dr. Duboise they take many amnesia patients on that basis. So you see, there's nothing to stop you from getting the best treatment available. And I'll be close enough to make sure you're staying out of trouble."

She searched his face and felt all the fight go out of her body. Was he making her an idle promise? She couldn't tell. What if he left her there alone for heaven only knew how long? For the first time, she considered the possibility that he might not want to have anything to do with her once he found out who she truly was.

She wondered if he'd been thinking the same thing and was making this move to get her out of his life before the truth came out.

"All right," she said stiffly. "Whatever you say."

Chapter Four

Trish checked into the hospital with a small valise of new clothes and personal effects that Andrew had insisted upon purchasing. She'd offered him her watch to pawn, but he had refused.

"Your credit's good with me. I'll just add the purchases to your running tab of three nights lodging and gourmet meals," he teased, but his levity had failed to lessen the tension between them. He'd been prepared for her backing out even as they made the drive to the hospital. She sat stiffly in the car, looking straight ahead, and barely nodding to acknowledge his attempt at making conversation.

When they had arrived at Havengate, he shot anxious glances at her pallid face to see how she was reacting to the cluster of pink stucco buildings that were scattered on the landscaped grounds, looking very much like a small college campus. He knew she felt betrayed by his insistence that she leave his house and check into the hospital. He only hoped that the decision would prove to be the right one, and, in time, she would thank him for it. He would do everything he could to make sure she didn't feel abandoned.

"What do you think, Trish?" he asked, acutely

needing reassurance that she didn't feel he'd stabbed her in the back.

"It looks—" she tried to find the right word.

"Safe?" he supplied, hopefully.

She managed a wan smile. "Yes, safe."

His anxious expression had made her lie. She felt anything but safe as she got out of the car, and waited for him to take her small bag out of the back seat. If there'd been anywhere to run to, she would have taken off in a flash.

As if reading her mind, he said gently. "Easy does it, Trish. If you hate the place, we'll find something different. Okay?"

"I hate it."

He laughed and shook his head. "Not so fast. How about a forty-eight-hour trial?"

"Okay, forty-eight hours."

Andrew slipped his arm through hers as they walked together into the main building, and she drew strength from the length of his warm firm body brushing hers. She wondered how she could bear to be parted from him for even the two days that she'd promised to stay.

Andrew held his breath that everything would go quickly and smoothly at registration. He had called ahead and talked with Dr. Duboise. The doctor had assured him that everything would be ready for Trish's admittance.

A pleasant middle-aged woman at the reception desk nodded when Andrew gave his name. "Oh, yes, Mr. Davis. We've been expecting you." She smiled at Trish, and put out her hand. "I'm Ms. Sloan. We have a nice room all ready for you, Trish."

The use of her name and the warm clasp of the woman's hand sent a momentary flicker of relief through Trish. She had expected to be treated like some poor victim who couldn't remember who she was instead of a person with all her faculties.

"Would you like to look over the premises before you settle in?" Ms. Sloan asked in an easy, friendly manner.

Andrew decided that the question must be a routine one. Apparently it was the hospital's policy to give people a chance to change their minds, he thought, holding his breath as he searched Trish's face to see what her response was going to be. Would she take advantage of the momentary reprieve and head back to the car?

Fortunately, there was only a slight hesitation before she said, "No, thank you. I'd rather go to my room."

"Fine." Ms. Sloan smiled. "If you'll follow me, please. It's just a short walk across the grounds to your building."

Andrew kept his arm through Trish's as they followed a sidewalk that led them to a two-storied pink stucco building that looked every bit like a college dormitory.

"You have room 110," Ms. Sloan told them as she opened a door on the first floor and motioned them inside.

Trish was surprised at the homey charm of the room, and its generous size. There was nothing of a sterile institution about the accommodations. Furnishings were in shades of a restful pink and green. Soft pillows brightened two lounge chairs and a single bed, which was covered with a pastel floral skirt and harmonizing bedspread. An adjoining bathroom was small with cream-colored fixtures and ceramic tiles.

"This building is close to the physical therapy and

occupational therapy departments,'' Ms. Sloan told Trish with a smile as if she were a social director acquainting a guest with all the offered accommodations. ''Dr. Duboise will be by later to get acquainted and set up a time for daily therapy.'' She pointed out a telephone on a small desk. ''If there's anything you need, just lift the receiver.'' She paused. ''Do you have any questions?''

Trish suppressed the impulse to reply that at the moment questions were all she had. She simply shook her head. ''No.''

Responding to the lost look in Trish's eyes, Ms. Sloan reached out and touched Trish's hand. ''We're a friendly bunch, Trish. You're going to like us. I promise.''

The pinched lines around Trish's mouth eased and she gave the woman a grateful smile. ''Thank you.''

''I'll leave you then,'' she said.

Andrew held out his hand. ''Thank you, Ms. Sloan.'' He was deeply grateful to her. She had offered Trish a reassurance that went beyond just professional concern.

She nodded and left them alone in the room.

Trish slowly walked over to a large window that overlooked plantings of flowers, trees and an expanse of emerald grass. Very deliberately, she drew the drapes, shutting out the view. Then she turned to Andrew. ''I can handle it from here.''

The dismissing edge of her tone cut him to the quick. As she stood there in the shadows of the darkened room, she looked like a child trying to hide from the world.

He moved quickly to her side. ''Don't be frightened. It's going to be all right.''

She lowered her head to keep him from seeing tears spilling from the corner of her eyes.

"I'm going to be here for you," he promised. He gently eased back strands of hair falling over her face and tucked them behind her ears. Then he gently cupped her chin, and lifted her face upward. He had intended to say something reassuring but the words got lost. A swell of emotions that made him a stranger to himself caused him to bend his head and kiss her.

Her mouth tensed under his, and for a second it seemed as if she were going to pull away. Then her arms crept up around his neck, and the kiss deepened until they both were breathless. Slowly, they withdrew from their heated embrace, and Andrew searched her face as she turned away from him and sat down on the edge of the bed.

How could he explain the wild impulse that had ignited such a passionate kiss? If he did try to explain, would he only make matters worse? He was angry with himself for taking advantage of her vulnerable emotions at a time like this.

"Trish, I—"

"Don't say anything," she pleaded. She couldn't stand hearing his apology for something that was her fault. If she hadn't behaved like a fearful child begging to be comforted, he never would have kissed her. *He feels sorry for me.* "Just let it go."

He started to protest, but he was stopped by the sudden appearance of a doctor in the open door. He was a short, robust man with a nicely trimmed black mustache that gave his round face a rather jaunty air.

"Dr. Duboise," he introduced himself as he came in, shaking hands with Andrew, and smiling at Trish. "Are you getting settled in?"

Trish gave him a noncommittal nod, and braced herself. The doctor's quick glance at the closed curtains and the shadowy cast to the room had already alerted her that nothing was going to get by him.

"I was just leaving," Andrew said quickly as he took Trish's cold hand in his. "You have my number. Call me, anytime." There were a dozen more things he wanted to say, but he settled for, "I'll be back tomorrow after work."

He felt her stiffen for a second as he leaned over and kissed her on the forehead. No doubt, the trained eye of the psychiatrist caught it all, Andrew thought as he left the room. Maybe Duboise would ask Trish what was going on between them—as if either of them knew!

Dr. Duboise settled in one of the easy chairs near where Trish sat on the edge of the bed. She expected him to turn on a light, but he didn't. As if reading her thoughts, he commented, "You find it more peaceful with the curtains drawn?"

"I find it safer," she answered flatly.

"Why safer?" There was no judgment in the question, just a quiet invitation, and it seemed to offer her a refuge for her thread-worn thoughts.

Slowly, she got up from the bed and sat down in the lounge chair that was placed close to his. As she met his steady eyes, she began talking, trying to put into words the nebulous sense of danger and apprehension that was like a bone-deep chill running through her as she tried to remember who she was and what had happened to her.

ANDREW WAS TRYING TO settle down at his computer and get some work done that evening when the telephone rang. Both relief and apprehension flooded through him when he heard Trish's voice on the line. He'd been wanting to call her, but hesitated because he wasn't certain what he should say to her. Remembering their passionate kiss and the way they'd melted together in that hot embrace made him cautious about upsetting her again.

"I just wanted to say good-night," she said in a soft voice.

"I'm glad you did. I've been thinking about you. How's it going?"

"I'm not sure," she admitted. "But I do feel better having told someone the whole story."

"You like Dr. Duboise, then?"

"Yes, I do. He just listened, and didn't give me the third degree. I was relieved that he didn't treat me like someone who is sick. He seemed to accept my paranoia as natural, under the circumstances."

Andrew let out a breath of relief. He had been wondering what to do if Trish absolutely refused to stay at Havengate. "I know he has a good reputation."

"He shared with me some of the scientific facts about amnesia that I didn't know. Maybe he was just doing a PR number on me, but he was hopeful that it was just a matter of time before my memory would return—little by little or all at once. I'm scheduled for a complete checkup in the morning to rule out any physical causes." She paused, not knowing how to apologize for her angry behavior toward him. "I'm indebted to you, Andrew. You were right to bring me here."

"I'm just relieved that things are going so well." Then he added impulsively, "But to tell the truth, I was wishing you were here so we could have another song fest.'' He didn't add that the ambiance of the whole house had changed in the three days she had spent with him. Everywhere he turned, in the kitchen, on the patio, and in his bedroom, there was a lingering aura of her presence.

''Maybe it's better I left when I did,'' she said quietly.

''Trish.'' He knew what she was thinking. ''I want to apologize for this afternoon. I really can't explain what happened—''

''You kissed me. Let's let it go at that. No need to make an issue out of it.'' She wasn't about to invite any expression of regret on his part. If she hadn't been so needy, he wouldn't have been drawn into the unexpected intimacy. How could she blame him for responding when she practically threw herself into his arms, and invited his kisses. She was totally embarrassed by what had happened, and was determined that it wasn't going to alienate his friendship.

Her curt rejection of his apology was reassuring in a way. Of course, she was right not to give an impulsive kiss any importance. The sooner forgotten the better, he told himself, but he'd never experienced such a surge of desire before. Forgetting it might not be as easy as he hoped.

''So I'll see you tomorrow evening, after work. Maybe we can have dinner together if they have a guest dining room.''

''I'd like that,'' she assured him, and an instant quickening of anticipation flowed through her. ''Heaven knows what the food will taste like, but I guess we can take our chances. And you could bring your guitar and play me another tune.''

''And you could sing—''

"And we could put out a hat for a collection."

"Sounds good to me," he agreed, laughing. "We'll split the earnings fifty-fifty."

She was smiling when she hung up, and gathered his old robe closer around her. Andrew had wanted to buy her some new night clothes, but she had insisted on bringing his sweatshirt and robe. They were the only things in her frightening situation that had any familiarity attached to them. Even though she knew that it wasn't wise to make him her whole world, she felt warm and comforted wearing his things.

SHE HAD LITTLE TIME the next day to think about anything but getting through myriad examinations and tests. Every inch of her body was scanned, poked and charted. She held up pretty well under the intense physical scrutiny, and wasn't surprised when Dr. Duboise gave her the results.

"We didn't find any injury to your head. The tenderness you told us about must have only been a bruise. There's no sign of any concussion."

"So what does that mean?"

"We're not dealing with any physical damage that has resulted in a loss of memory. A blow to the head might have triggered the amnesia, but, in your case, is not the cause of it."

"Is that good?"

He smiled and nodded. "Your brain is in A-one condition. Your loss of memory is most likely due to a desire to dissociate from a particularly intolerable situation."

Intolerable situation.

"I can't remember because I don't want to?"

"That's about it. This kind of amnesia can cause

personal memories, like your identity, to be temporary lost, while cognitive skills like language and learned behavior remain intact.''

He talked for a few minutes about the different locations in the brain for various functions, but Trish only half listened. Her overriding concern was the prognosis for getting her memory back.

''Good,'' he assured her when she asked. ''Try to relax and go with the program we have set out for you. Trying to force yourself to remember doesn't remove any of the road blocks. You may recover your memory all at once, or you may experience just bits of memory, and our job will be to piece them together like a jigsaw puzzle.''

''I hate puzzles,'' Trish said without thinking, and then looked startled. ''How did I know that?''

Dr. Duboise chuckled. ''Don't worry about it. Just accept it. You're going to be a prize patient. I can tell.''

When Andrew arrived that evening, Trish was keyed up, anxious to tell him about her day. They had a pleasant, no-frills dinner in a spacious cafeteria, and then took a leisurely walk around the grounds.

''I spent a couple of hours in the physical therapy department,'' she told him with an eagerness that gave a lift to her voice. ''Guess what? The therapist said that I must be dedicated to regular exercise because I have excellent muscle tone. Isn't that something? He put me through some pretty vigorous routines and I did really well.''

''That's great,'' Andrew said, delighted at her high spirits. Certainly anything positive that she discovered about herself was a blessing, and he wondered if it had been her physical stamina that had saved her life.

There was an animated energy that he hadn't seen before.

"Guess what the occupational therapist said after looking carefully at my manicured nails and soft hands?"

"You're a lady of leisure, or someone who doesn't do any physical chores?"

"That's close enough. She told me we'd concentrate on finding out what kind of tastes and hobbies I might have. The room was filled with people painting, drawing, some working with clay, others knitting or sitting at sewing machines. None of the activities made any kind of a call to me, but when I told her that I liked music, she said we'd start there." She gave her head a toss. "It isn't much, but it's a start."

He was delighted with her unexpected transformation. There was an energy about her that even made her more appealing. He hadn't been able to get her out of his mind all day, and had been prepared to deal with pleas to let her go back to his place. All of his mental arguments were a waste of time—at least for the moment. He didn't know if her present attitude would hold up in the face of a prolonged disappointment, but he felt as if a great hurdle had been safely passed.

"I'm going to lick this thing," she told him, even as she tried to still the quivering fears that lay beneath the words.

When he told her, "Good night," at her door, he lightly kissed her on the forehead. It was a benign gesture, void of any kind of passion or desire. "I'll be working at home tomorrow. Call me if you run out of something to do, or someone to talk with."

She saw that his arms were dropped passively at his

side, and she felt that he'd taken several steps away from her even though he hadn't moved. His expression was friendly, and nothing more. She remembered the warmth of his embrace, but he made no effort to draw her closer. *Well, what did you expect?* an inner voice mocked. He was obviously relieved that she wasn't making a fuss to get out of this place.

"Thanks, but I think they're going to keep me rather busy," she said, determined to let him off the hook. She'd messed his life up enough already.

Andrew's feelings were mixed as he drove back home. Certainly he was glad to see that Trish was determined to come to grips with her lost memory, but a part of him regretted that she no longer needed his support. He wished that they'd talked about the momentary sexual tension that had flared between them. He'd never been adept at handling confrontations. Because of his insecurity as a foster child, his way was to let things ride, and hope that misunderstandings would work themselves out, but in this situation time might be an enemy. He could feel the door closing on him with every piece of her memory that returned. She had brought into his life a glimpse of the kind of companionship that he'd been missing. How ironic, he thought, that the woman who had broken into his solitary shell was someone who didn't even know who she was.

THE NEXT FEW DAYS PASSED without incident. Andrew worked at home and visited Trish in the evening. The exuberance of her first day had faded. On the fourth night, she'd experienced another one of the fearful nightmares.

"Dr. Duboise says it's a good thing." She told Andrew as she suppressed a tremor. "Something in my subconscious is trying to come to the surface. Maybe when it does, I'll remember everything."

Andrew didn't tell her that he'd been endeavoring to find some clue to her identity on his own, but had come up empty-handed. Because he'd honored his promise not to publicize her story or whereabouts, keeping her situation a secret was like tying his hands behind his back. He read all the stories he could find about people reported missing.

And then one noon hour, it happened. He had spread out a collection of papers on the table as he sat in his usual booth, eating his lunch. A bite of sandwich caught in his throat when he turned a page in *The New York Times,* and glanced over the news stories. He wasn't prepared for the victory that met his eyes, and he read a small news item in disbelief.

"Memorial service to be held for missing prominent New York investor and Realtor. Ms. Patricia Louise Radcliffe, a wealthy businesswoman and socialite, disappeared during the height of the recent storm. She is believed to have been in the company of her partner, Perry Reynolds, who is also missing."

The article was accompanied by a fashionable photograph showing a smiling Trish, her hair beautifully styled, a jeweled necklace circling her slender neck. She was wearing an off the shoulder gown, cutting daringly low to show the soft crevice between her full breasts.

As he looked at the photo, her eyes seemed to hold a sardonic smile, as if she appreciated the trick that fate had played on him.

Chapter Five

Andrew kept staring at Trish's picture with emotions that defied definition. Excitement was there, and relief, too, but there was also regret, chagrin and disappointment. Even though he had suspected Trish came from an affluent lifestyle, he wasn't prepared for the fact that she belonged in a world of high finance and money. At the back of his mind had been the hope that maybe, just maybe, there might be a continuing relationship after they discovered her identity, but he knew now that such a hope was romantic nonsense. Once she was drawn back into her own world, her emotional need for a hermit loner would be over.

He read the article over several times, trying to decide the best way to handle the matter. Dr. Duboise would have be told first. The doctor would be the best one to give Trish the news that she was Ms. Patricia Radcliffe of New York City.

TRISH WAS IN THE physical therapy room, working on an exercise machine, when a secretary from Dr. Duboise's office informed her that the doctor would like to see her.

"I've already had my therapy session this morning,'' Trish replied, puzzled. Just the way the woman was looking at her created an instant quiver of uneasiness. ''What does he want?''

''He wants to talk with you.''

''What about?''

She hesitated. ''I'm not sure.''

The woman was lying, Trish was certain of it. Had the hospital decided they couldn't keep her after all? Obviously, treatment was expensive and she'd made no progress at all in recovering her memory in the week she'd been there.

''All right. I'll shower and be in his office in about fifteen minutes.''

Her mind whirled as she walked slowly across the grounds from her room to Duboise's office. What had she said during the morning session that made him want to see her again? If she was released from Havengate, where would she go? Should she ask Andrew to let her come back? Even though a deep seated, lurking fear remained just below her consciousness, and she felt the cottage was a safe sanctuary, she knew that it wasn't fair to him to disrupt his life along with her own.

''Come in, Trish,'' Duboise greeted her with a smile, which put Trish more on edge than ever. She didn't trust his smooth manner. There was an energy about him that radiated a warning. He motioned to a large burgundy armchair where she always sat during their sessions.

She sat down stiffly, clutching her hands together. ''What is this all about? What's wrong?''

''Nothing's wrong,'' he assured her with his usual easy smile as he leaned back in his chair.

''Then why am I here again today?''

"Trish, I want you to try and relax. Take a deep breath and let it out slowly. Another one. Another. All right. Now close your eyes. I'm going to say a name for you."

She instantly stiffened instead of relaxing. *What name?* Her nails dug into her palms.

"Keep breathing deeply, Trish. Just let this name float in your mind like a petal moving on water." He said the name softly. "Patricia Louise Radcliffe." He repeated it two more times, and then waited.

Trish mouthed the name without any recognition, but when she opened her eyes, and saw the way he was looking at her, she knew why he had brought her to his office. He had expected her to recognize the name, but it was no more familiar than the names of missing persons that Andrew had given her.

Strangely enough she hated to disappoint the doctor more than she felt any deep emotion herself. She had already suffered too many disappointments, and spent too many long hours trying to find a glimmer of remembrance in the world around her.

"I'm sorry," she said, knowing that she had dashed his hopes by her lack of response.

"Close your eyes again, Trish. Breathe deeply. Relax." After a moment, he said again, "Let this name float gently in your mind. Perry Reynolds. Perry Reynolds."

She jerked in shock as if an electric current had charged through her. For a second, she saw a man's face clearly, graying dark hair, round features and blue eyes. Then the face was lost in a kaleidoscope of images and sounds that whirled in a vertigo of thundering water, crashing timbers and shadowy shapes.

She put her hand to her throat, cried out, gasping

for air as if the whirling visions in her head were strangling her.

"You're all right, Trish. You're all right." Dr. Duboise bent over her, speaking in a soothing tone.

She leaned back in the chair, limp and drained. After a moment, she managed to ask in a breathless voice, "Who is Perry Reynolds?"

He avoided answering her for a moment, and instead asked her some open-ended questions about what she had seen and felt when the images flashed before her. When he was satisfied that she'd shared everything as best as she could, he leaned over and took her hand.

"I got a call from your friend, Andrew Davis, about an hour ago, and he sent me a fax of a newspaper article about a memorial service being held for a woman who was presumed lost in the recent storm."

"Patricia Radcliffe?"

He nodded and as his steady gaze met hers, she knew that he was convinced that she was this person. Suddenly having a strange name thrust upon her was almost as frightening as not knowing her identity at all.

"And Andrew thought the woman might be me?" She shook her head in disbelief. "It can't be. The name doesn't mean anything. It must be somebody else." She refused to let them shove somebody else's identity on her. "It has to be."

He handed her the newspaper, and said gently, "That's your picture, isn't it?"

She stared at the photograph and her likeness as if it would fade under her disbelieving scrutiny. "Patricia Louise Radcliffe." She mouthed the name under the picture, and then, with a sense of frightening detachment, she read the article.

"Perry Reynolds." Her lips quivered. She was bewildered why his name had brought more of an emotional response than hearing her own name. "Why do I remember his name and what he looked like, and I can't remember my own?"

Dr. Duboise shook his head. "I don't know, Trish. But I'm confident that one of these days you'll tell me."

ANDREW LEFT WORK EARLY, too keyed up to get any work of his own done. When he'd returned to the office after lunch, he'd contacted Dr. Duboise, and then used the Internet to glean some information about Atlantis Enterprises, the company that Patricia had inherited from her late father, Winston Radcliffe. The following year she had created a partnership with Perry Reynolds and the assets of the company were worth several million dollars. Andrew stared at reports that listed a staggering net worth for both partners.

When he realized fully that Patricia Radcliffe was the woman who had been sleeping in his lumpy bed and wearing his faded clothes, he felt like someone who had been the butt of a very poor joke.

When Andrew arrived at Havengate later that afternoon, Trish was in her room, lying on the bed and staring at the ceiling. He knocked softly on the open door, and she sat up quickly.

"Andrew," she gasped. "Thank God, you've come. Tell me what to do. I must be this Patricia Radcliffe person, but I don't even know her. How can I take over the life of someone when her name doesn't even seem familiar?"

"Hey, take it easy. No need to panic," he said in a gentle, reassuring tone.

"It's not true. I'm not that person."

Andrew looked at her in disbelief. He had expected that once Trish learned her identity, there would be some kind of a breakthrough in her memory, but if the name meant nothing to her, she was still as much in the dark as ever. "Patricia Radcliffe doesn't mean anything to you at all?"

"It's a name, that's all. I don't have any sense that it belongs to me. That news item was like reading about someone else."

"You don't remember anything?" he asked as he sat down on the bed beside her. She was wearing the inexpensive white shorts and simple summer top that he had bought for her.

"Yes, I did have a momentary recall." Her lips trembled. "When I heard the name Perry Reynolds, a sudden image of a man flashed in my mind for a split second. The article said he was her business partner."

Andrew noted that she said, *her business partner,* not my business partner.

"When Dr. Duboise said his name, the image of a graying dark-haired man with a round face flashed across my mind. And I heard horrible sounds of thunder and roaring water."

She shivered and Andrew's arm went around her waist. "But that's wonderful, Trish. Don't you see? It's a beginning."

Her anxious gaze dragged across his face. "The paper said this man is missing, too. Do you think this Perry Reynolds is the one making me afraid to remember who I am?"

Andrew was wondering the same thing, but he knew

better than to indulge in any idle speculation. "What does Dr. Duboise say?"

"He warned me about jumping to any conclusions, but I can't help it." She leaned her head against his shoulder and he tightened his embrace. "It's really strange. I was almost tempted to show up at that memorial service, just as an on-looker. What do think would have happened if I'd walked in on the service?"

"Oh, maybe a half-dozen people would have fainted away." He knew she was serious, but he decided to make light of it.

"Dr. Duboise said he would alert the authorities that I'd been located, so they'll call off the service, but no information would be given as to my whereabouts."

"Good." He was relieved that she wasn't going to be immediately bombarded with a lot of strange people rushing at her. "That will give you time to decide how you want to handle all of this."

"I suppose so," she said thoughtfully.

He was ready to answer as many questions as he could about Atlantis Enterprises, but, surprisingly enough, she didn't even mention the company. Apparently, none of the details of Patricia Radcliffe's business life had any relevancy for her at the moment.

"I've read the article over and over again, but my mind is still blank." She fell silent for a long moment and then she straightened up. "Do you think we could get out of here for a couple of hours?"

"Sure. Where would you like to go?" he asked, at once surprised and pleased. Was she really ready to show herself out in public? Dr. Duboise had given his permission for her to leave the premises with him.

"Could we go to your place?"

He was startled by the rush of pleasure that made

him answer quickly, "Sure. We'll stop and get something to eat on the deck. How about Chinese?"

"Perfect."

She said little on the drive to his house, but the silence between them was comfortable, and Andrew was grateful for it. He liked to think things through before expressing his opinions, and he was certain that the conversation would eventually turn to what she should do next.

All afternoon, he'd been trying to coordinate what he knew about Trish's situation and the information presented in the newspaper. There was no doubt that she had disappeared during the storm. That was a given because of the time he had found her. There seemed to be some question about whether or not she was in the company of her business partner, Perry Reynolds. Now that Andrew knew about the sudden flash of Trish's memory of the man's face, and the accompanying noises, he was ready to believe that her business partner had been with her in the storm. But how had she ended up on his beach alone?

Andrew sensed that Trish was as tight as bowstrings when they reached his house, so he suggested a stroll on the beach before enjoying the various cartons of Chinese food. Trish readily agreed.

A late afternoon sun brushed the ocean with a glitter of diamonds as it sent shafts of light through soft clouds collecting on the horizon. A wild flutter of seagulls darting over the water mingled with the soft ebbing and flowing of the surf upon the sand.

Trish and Andrew walked in the opposite direction of the cove, and as he glanced at her face lifted to the evening breeze, a sudden sense of sadness descended upon him. This might be the last time that they would be together like this, but in a strange way, she had somehow become his, and he wished that there had been no newspaper article to take her away from him. He put his arm around her waist as they walked, as if he could somehow claim her. She smiled up at him, and as he looked into her sweet face, he wanted to trace the soft curve of her cheeks with his fingertips, and bury his lips in the smooth loveliness of her neck. And more than that—he wanted the impossible—he wanted to keep her in his life.

When they saw a group of young people having a beach party just ahead, Trish slowed her steps and instantly stiffened. "I think we ought to go back." *What if they know me?* The thought raced across her mind before she caught herself.

"All right," Andrew said, but before they could turn around to retrace their steps, a volleyball came from out of nowhere and almost hit him. His reflexes were quick enough to grab it. A rather chubby girl with flying red hair came running toward them.

"Great catch!" she squealed. "Reinforcements! Just in time, too. I'm down two on my team. Come on, we'll show 'em how it's done. There's an extra piece of pie riding on this match."

She grabbed Trish's hand. "So glad you could come. I'm Dee," she said, laughing.

Trish looked at her speechless, and before Andrew could explain to the vivacious redhead that there had been some mistake, his words were lost in a clamor of several enthusiastic players who surrounded them and urged them toward a volleyball net.

"Way to go, Dee."

"Keeping the best in reserve, were you?"

Andrew searched Trish's face. How was she reacting to all of this? He half-expected her to turn and run, but her initial apprehension faded into an expression of surprised wonderment. The warm acceptance of the young people seemed to be having a healing effect on her, and she didn't protest when she and Andrew were drawn along with everyone else back to volleyball net.

"You serve," Dee told Andrew who still had the ball in his hands.

"I'll do it," Trish spoke up. Andrew stared at her, not sure that the words had come from her mouth. "I'll serve," she repeated.

"All right."

He handed her the ball, and she turned it over in her hand as if getting acquainted with an old friend. Her eyes held a sudden eager glint that startled him. Then she walked to the correct position and lifting her head, she tossed up the ball and sent it over the net with devastating force and precision.

"Way to go," Dee squealed when the other team failed to return the fast serve.

Andrew couldn't hide his astonishment. She was good. Really good. Where had she learned to play like that? He loved the way her agile body moved with polished grace, light and sure. Her quickness and aptitude in returning balls soon made her the most accomplished player in the group. When the other team lost by a huge margin they put up a howl.

"Not fair. Not fair."

"You brought in a professional ringer!"

"Where'd you learn to serve like that?"

"I honestly don't know," she said, laughing, surprised at herself. For the first time she was able to make light of her lost memory. "I don't remember."

Her face was flushed and her eyes bright, and Andrew glimpsed the young girl who had played volleyball with such vigor and joy. He wondered if her youth had been cut short by the responsibilities and expectations that, obviously, had fallen on her shoulders at a young age.

"Time to eat," Dee announced as she hooked one of her plump arms through Trish's and offered the other one to Andrew. "And the winning team gets to line up first."

Andrew shot a questioning look at Trish. Her hair was moist with sweat beaded on her forehead, and a healthy glow had replaced her former pallor. She didn't look as if she needed rescuing, but he wasn't sure. He was a little uneasy about her sudden metamorphosis from a frightened recluse to the center of attention.

"What do you think?" he asked, cautiously.

She smiled at him. "Would you mind? I mean, you could save the Chinese food...." Her voice trailed off.

"No problem. We'll have it another night," he promised, returning her smile, but even as he spoke, there was an inner warning that there might not be another night like this. Once her true identity claimed her, there seemed little likelihood they would be crashing any more beach parties.

Nobody seemed interested in asking Trish and Andrew who they were or why they had joined the party. They sat with the others around a fire, roasting hot dogs and marshmallows and loading their plates with salad and slices of berry pie. The flow of laughter, good humor and open acceptance circled them like welcoming arms.

As twilight thickened, someone brought out a guitar

and Trish whispered to Andrew, "You play better than that."

He put his arm around her and she settled back against him. Both of them were content to hold on to this moment in time, a blessed eternity if only for a few hours.

When the party broke up they walked in silence back to the cottage. It was still a lovely warm night, and the ocean reflected a blanket of shimmering stars. Their steps were slow and reluctant as they neared the cottage.

"Would you like a cup of coffee before I take you back?" Andrew asked, knowing that he was guilty of trying to hold on to the evening as long as possible.

"Do I have to go back?" she asked, knowing the answer before he nodded. Sighing, she sat down at the patio table. "Maybe if I stay out too late, they'll kick me out."

"Not a chance. But they might not let me on the grounds again."

When he returned with two steaming mugs, he found her leaning forward with her head in her hands. The look she gave him when she raised her head told him the brief reprieve she'd had from the ordeal facing her was over.

He sat down on a bench facing her. He didn't trust himself to get too close. At the slightest invitation, he would have taken her in his arms, and given into the desire to forget about everything but making love to her. He knew that under the circumstances, he wouldn't be able to live with himself if he let that happen. Living with regret was something he chose not to put on either of them.

"Would you like to talk about it?" he asked quietly.

At first, he thought she hadn't even heard him, but then she gave a small jerk and moistened her dry lips.

"Yes, I would. I don't like to burden you with all of this." Then she gave him a feeble smile. "But I guess it's a little late for that."

"You haven't been a burden. Whatever happens, I want you to know that. I'll support any decision that you make," he promised. *Even if it ends up tearing me apart.*

"I don't see any way to escape what must be done—now or later. If I try to postpone the inevitable, it is only going to keep me in constant dread. Tonight made me realize how important it is for me to be me. Hiding myself away isn't going solve anything, is it?"

"I'm afraid not." He didn't add that there was little chance of keeping her anonymity for very long once the word was out that she was still alive. Someone with Patricia Radcliffe's reputation and past visibility would invite public attention. Sooner or later, whatever lay out there, waiting for her, would have to be faced.

Her hands tightened around the mug as she set it down on the patio table. "I'm still scared."

"I know. And you have every right to be. But it's going to be all right. You're a strong person, Trish. And you're very capable. You can lick this thing. I know you can."

"But what if I can't? What if I find out I don't like Patricia Louise Radcliffe?"

He forgot about keeping his distance, and moved quickly beside her on the bench. "Then you don't have to be her. You can change."

"But what if I can't?" She looked up into his eyes and added in a frightened whisper, "What if someone won't let me?"

Chapter Six

Patricia Radcliffe lived in a fashionable high-rise building on Central Park West. Her home was on the twelfth floor overlooking the street and park, and all the staff in the building had been advised of her arrival.

As Andrew and Trish emerged from the cab that had brought them from Havengate into the city, a middle-aged doorman in a gold-braided uniform stepped forward and tipped his hat.

"Welcome back, Ms. Radcliffe," he greeted her with an expression that was both warm and speculative.

"Thank you," Trish responded but her voice was thin and unsure. *Should I know him?*

"I'm Harold Wills, ma'am," he added when her return smile was hesitant and unsure. "I've been your doorman for nigh on fifteen years."

Fifteen years, and she felt as if she'd never seen him before in her life.

"I'm sorry. I—"

"That's all right. I understand," he said quickly, and the look he gave her was one of kindly pity.

She wanted to turn and run before a battery of unfamiliar people lined up in front of her, and demanded impatiently, "Of course, you remember me."

Her instinct for flight communicated itself to Andrew. He firmly took her arm, guiding her past the doorman and into a spacious foyer that was nearly as large as his whole cottage. Modern style furniture, mirrored walls and art-deco furnishings appeared to be more for looks than offering any invitation to linger, thought Andrew. He wondered if anyone except the doorman ever dared to spend any time there.

Keeping close to Trish, they walked across the marble floor to two elevators that faced the front door. A light was on in one, advising them that it was descending from the tenth floor. Andrew quickly punched a different button and was thankful when the second elevator flew open immediately. He could tell Trish was about to bolt.

"Here we go," he said in an encouraging tone, keeping a guiding hand on her arm as he ushered her into the spacious carpeted elevator. Trish gave a small shudder as the doors closed quietly and the cage began to lift.

"It's going to be all right," he said softly. "Remember what Dr. Duboise said. Don't put yourself under any pressure to remember anyone or anything. Just take it as it comes. If something seems familiar, admit it. If it doesn't, don't feel that you have to lie. These people are your friends."

Are they? Why did she feel that she was about to line up in front of a firing squad? Trish silently asked herself.

They stepped out on the twelfth floor into a spacious corridor. A small decorative table holding an elaborate artificial floral arrangement was flanked by two small brocaded chairs which Andrew guessed were provided for anyone who wanted to sit while waiting for the elevator to arrive.

Trish looked up and down the hall, stared at decorative double doors facing them, and read a small brass holder displaying the name, Patricia Radcliffe. None of it seemed the least bit familiar to her.

"I'm not ready for this." A spurt of panic sent her heart racing, and she tried to stop Andrew from ringing the doorbell. "Let's go. Please, I can't do it." The words were no sooner out of her mouth when the door swung open.

"I thought I heard the elevator." A middle-aged, plump, brown-skinned woman in a housekeeper's navy blue dress smiled broadly at Trish. "We've been waiting for you, honey." Her anxious eyes traveled over Trish. "Are you all right? Goodness' sakes, you gave us a terrible fright."

"Sasha, let them in," a masculine voice ordered. A tall man dressed in an expensive Italian suit, chambray white shirt and silk tie appeared behind the housekeeper. He was in his thirties, his dark hair precisely styled around rather thin, chiseled features. His hazel eyes searched Trish's face as if wanting to reassure himself that her reappearance wasn't some hoax being played on them.

After a moment, his mouth quivered with suppressed emotion. "It's really you."

He started to reach out to her but Trish drew back, staring at him with an expression of someone meeting a forward stranger.

"And who are you?" she asked point-blank.

The expression on his face would have been laughable, thought Andrew, if it hadn't been so pathetic.

At that moment, a slender woman, thirtyish, with short frosted brown hair framing a pleasant face, appeared in the doorway of the living room.

"For heaven's sake, Curtis," she said briskly. "Don't leave them standing in the foyer." Her steady gaze traveled over Trish but she didn't rush forward or try to make conversation. "I'm Janelle," she said simply, and then led the way into a spacious room decorated as beautifully as any magazine spread.

Trish stood frozen in the middle of the floor, letting her gaze travel over the white carpet, brocade drapes and French Provincial style furniture. Large oil paintings were hung by gold chords in artistic arrangements on the walls.

If I really am Patricia Radcliffe, did I select the furnishings or hire an interior decorator? she asked herself. There was little evidence of any personal belongings in the ultra fashionable decor. As she stood there, nothing triggered any memory of the room, nor any of the many things that must have happened there.

She looked at Andrew with an expression of total bewilderment. "Does this seem like me?"

"I don't know," he said honestly. How could he know what her tastes were before they were wiped out with her memory?

"Welcome home, Patricia," Janelle said, obviously responding to Trish's utter bewilderment. "Please tell us what you'd like to have us do."

"I don't know," she answered honestly. She didn't know whether Janelle was another employee, a personal friend, or someone from the office.

"I'm Curtis Mandel," said the tall man as he stood stiffly in front of the fireplace, frowning at her.

"Curtis and I are both business associates of yours," Janelle explained.

"And close personal friends," Curtis added with a pointed look at Andrew. "Sir, we are a little confused about what part you played in this...unfortunate situation. You are...?"

"Andrew Davis," he answered without bothering to hold out his hand for a shake. The man's tone made it clear that this wasn't going to be a friendly introduction.

Aware of the hostility in the questions leveled at Andrew, Trish said quickly, "Andrew found me half-drowned on the beach."

"So we heard," Curtis said dryly. "And you didn't see anything that would help us understand what happened to Patricia or Perry to bring about this unfortunate condition, Mr. Davis?"

"No, I didn't," Andrew answered shortly, irritated at the man's skeptical tone. Did Curtis Mandel actually believed that he could be orchestrating this whole thing?

Andrew felt a healthy instant dislike for Curtis Mandel for more than one reason. The man had, undoubtedly, sized up Andrew's inexpensive sports jacket and trousers in one word—cheap. As Curtis moved to Trish's side, anyone could tell from the way he looked at Trish that his feelings for her were not all business. Andrew couldn't help but wonder if Patricia Radcliffe had returned those feelings.

"Patricia, darling, is it really true that you don't remember anything?" Curtis gently probed as he searched her pale face. "You must remember me. You do, don't you?"

Trish's anguished expression was answer enough,

and Janelle broke in impatiently. "For pity's sake, Curtis, don't give the poor girl the third degree two minutes after she's walked through the door. I'm sorry, Patricia. You'll have to be patient with us. No one can imagine what you're going through. What would make this whole thing easier for you?"

Trish caught her lower lip. *I'd like to go back to Andrew's place.* She sent him a pleading look, but he answered Janelle's question for her. "I think she'd probably like to have some time to herself to sort things out."

"Of course," Janelle agreed readily. "We want to do whatever's best for her. I'll try to head off the crowd of people who are likely to descend upon her the minute word gets out that she's home."

"I'm sure we can handle things from here," Curtis told Andrew in a dismissing tone. "Patricia has loyal friends who will protect her and see to her welfare."

The warning was so blatant that it made Andrew reply just as forcibly. "I'm sure she does— I'm one of them."

Janelle's amused glance took in the two men. "Well, now that we've got that settled, why don't we give Patricia some privacy? I'll bet she'd like to rest and get into some of her own clothes." She eyed the simple sundress that Andrew had bought for Trish. "I think a woman's wardrobe always helps her to identify herself."

If only it were that simple, Trish thought. Didn't Janelle realize outward trappings couldn't miraculously rescue her from a deep-seated memory loss? She knew the woman was doing her best to cope with this awkward situation, and Trish had the feeling she was as much a friend as a business associate.

At that moment the doorbell rang, and the housekeeper, Sasha, who had been hovering at the back of room listening to the conversation, hurriedly went to answer it.

Both Janelle and Curtis stiffened as they heard voices and a woman's sharp question, "Is she here?"

Trish gasped as a faint flicker of recognition almost rose to the surface. *That voice!* Did she know it? As she fixed her gaze on the living room door, her knees suddenly felt ready to give way. Andrew touched her shoulder and she gained strength from his warm squeeze.

Sasha led two people into the room, a curvaceous blond woman wearing a tight sexy crimson dress, and a young man somewhere in his twenties who looked about ten years her junior. They stopped just inside the room and stared at Trish as if she were some apparition suddenly appearing from the dead.

Trish didn't remember either of them.

"There you are," the woman said in her loud, breezy voice. "I can't believe it. This whole thing has been a dreadful nightmare. I want some answers, Patricia, right now."

The young man grabbed her arm. "Take it easy, Darlene."

"Shut up, Gary," she snapped, keeping her demanding eyes fixed on Trish. "Tell me, what happened to Perry? Where is he? I want the truth, Patricia. No more of this sneaking around behind my back."

"For godsake, Darlene," Janelle snapped, "this is no time to go into your paranoia tirade."

"Paranoia, is it?" she scoffed. "The two of them sneaked off on an afternoon rendezvous, I just know it. And they took advantage of the storm to make us all crazy with worry. I'm willing to bet that the two of them were cuddled up somewhere all this time, having a good laugh on all of us.'' She narrowed her heavy thick eyelashes, and then turned to Curtis. ''What kind of a story has she told you?''

''We haven't had a chance to talk,'' he answered sharply. ''But I agree with Janelle. You don't have any cause to throw around such malicious accusations.''

''Oh, you know my stepmother,'' the young man said with a sardonic smile as he flopped down in a chair. ''She creates her own soap operas, don't you, Mama, dear?''

Darlene sent him a glare that would have withered most people. ''We're not all as stupid as you are, Gary. Just because your father always bails you out of your miserable schemes doesn't make him a saint.'' Her eyes flashed back to Trish. ''Especially when there's a designing, manipulative woman around.''

''Are you referring to yourself by any chance, making these outlandish accusations?'' Andrew asked boldly. He could see that Trish was reeling under the onslaught of the woman's vitriolic insinuations, and he was ready to physically remove the obnoxious woman from the room.

''And who in the hell are you?'' Darlene demanded, turning on Andrew with flashing eyes.

''Our hero of the moment,'' Curtis answered dryly. ''Darlene Reynolds meet Andrew Davis. I was just asking him if he'd seen anything of your husband.''

''And?''

Curtis just shrugged.

''Enough of this!'' Trish snapped. From some deep well of latent strength, she found the courage to take charge, and speak her mind. "I don't remember any of you. And at the moment, that seems to be a blessing."

Andrew gave her an approving grin.

I have a temper. Good, for me, she thought. At least, she wasn't afraid of the present situation anymore. Pent-up feelings of paranoia that she'd been harboring seemed to fade in this face-to-face meeting with the people in her life. She felt more than capable of handling any of them. "Right now, I want all of you except Andrew to get out of here and leave me alone."

"I don't think that's a good idea, Patricia," Curtis responded in a conciliatory tone. "At the very least, Janelle should stay. She'll be able to help you orient yourself in the apartment, and run interference with unwanted visitors." He didn't add Janelle would also serve as chaperone, but the look he gave Andrew was clear enough.

"Maybe it would be best if I stayed, Patricia. Don't you think so, Andrew?" Janelle asked, looking at him for his approval.

He nodded, and lowering his voice, he said softly to Trish, "I'll come back later, after you've had a chance to settle in. You can always call me. The office is only a few minutes away. Okay, Trish?"

He searched her face, wanting to take her in his arms and tell everyone else to get the hell out of there. If there had been some way to spare her all of this, he would have jumped at it.

She drew in a deep breath, trying to still an impulse to beg him to stay—or take her with him. He was right, of course. Nothing would be gained by trying to run away. She had to know the truth about herself, even if the ugly things the malevolent blonde was saying about her were true.

"Good. Everyone but Janelle will clear out and give you time to reorient yourself."

"And who put you in charge, Mr. Whatever-your-name is?" Darlene snapped.

"I was wondering the same thing," Curtis said, his dark eyes narrowing. "Aren't you being a little presumptuous telling Patricia what to do? How long have you known her? A week? Maybe you ought to back off and let her old friends look after her."

"Just go, all of you," Trish ordered. "Now." She turned to Janelle. "Show me where my room is. I want to lie down."

Trish turned on her heel and started toward an open door leading off the living room.

"No, not that way." Janelle said quickly, stopping her. "That's the hall that leads to the library, dining room and kitchen. The hall to the bedrooms is this way." She looped her arm through Trish's. "I'll show you."

Trish gave her a grateful look and ignored the poignant silence that followed them out of the room.

After they had disappeared down the hall, the young man, Gary, smirked as he got to his feet. "Quite a performance. I felt like clapping."

"For once, I agree you with, Gary," said his stepmother said in a tone that indicated any agreement between them was a rarity. "It's obvious that this whole amnesia bit is a put-on."

"Oh, come on, Darlene," Curtis said impatiently. "Why would Patricia participate in such an elaborate hoax?"

"Don't be naive, Curtis," she snapped. "She was

always able to pull the wool over your eyes. Don't you see? She and Perry are trying to pull off some nefarious scheme to make more money, and keep every precious dollar for themselves.'' She glared at Andrew as she put her hands on her curvaceous hips in a challenging manner. ''I don't know what your part is in this con game, but it isn't going to work. I'm warning you. The authorities are going to get an earful from me.''

''Good,'' Andrew responded smoothly. ''I'm glad we have a meeting of the minds on this. We all want to know what really happened, don't we?''

As he let his gaze meet those of the three people facing him, he stiffened against a wave of apprehension. Did they know things that would fall together in a hard truth that would replace his captivating Trish with an unappealing Patricia Radcliffe?

THE BEAUTIFULLY FURNISHED bedroom didn't evoke a single strand of recognition as Trish hesitated just inside the door, and let her eyes travel around the room. She could have been visiting someone else's house, and if Janelle hadn't led her into this room, she might have made a mistake and chosen a different one.

A lovely embossed wallpaper in shades of cream and soft pink harmonized with floral curtains, a matching bedspread and ruffled pillows. A graceful chaise lounge was set in a corner near a bookshelf.

''You just had the room redecorated,'' Janelle offered, as if this fact might change Trish's blank expression to one of remembrance. ''Eloise at Sullivan Interiors did it. You spent a lot of time selecting the right swatches of material for the drapes, bedspread and rug.'' She smiled at Trish. ''You and Eloise had a few words about what you wanted, and what she thought you should have.''

The choice of colors and fabrics were clues that Trish embraced eagerly. *I like pastel colors, floral prints, and soft fabrics.* Yes, the bedroom seemed friendly and comfortable. ''I like it,'' she said with a sense of relief.

''Would you like to shower and change into some different clothes?'' Janelle asked in a tone which suggested that a change was in order.

Trish nodded. Like a person snooping into someone else's walk-in closet, she surveyed racks crowded with designer clothes. *Are all of these mine?* Cautiously, she studied some of the suits, dresses and evening clothes, hoping they would provide more personal information about herself. She even closed her eyes, trying to draw some fleeting images from them, but nothing would come to her. If she'd ever worn these clothes, nothing remained in her mind as an imprint of remembrance.

Janelle tried to be helpful. ''Do you remember this one?'' she asked Trish as she handed her a lovely peacock-blue dress.

Trish touched the shimmering cloth and let her fingertips trace its soft silken folds. The fabric was sensual to the touch, and the color captivating to the eyes. ''It's beautiful,'' she said softly.

''You bought it at Francine Originals the last time we went shopping. Just a week before...before you disappeared. We spent the whole day trying on dresses, going to the spa and beauty parlor.'' She sighed. ''I can't believe you've forgotten all the good times we've had together. Ever since I came to work at Atlantis, six years ago, we've been more than just business associates.'' Janelle's lips quivered as if she was struggling to hold back tears. ''We've been friends.''

Impulsively, Trish reached out and hugged her. ''I could use a good friend right now, Janelle.''

''Me, too. The office is in a mess ever since you've been gone. Curtis is throwing his weight around. Everyone is pointing a finger at someone else. My workload is doubled. I'm so glad you're back. I could always depend upon you to understand.''

They sat down on the edge of the bed together like two girlfriends sharing with each other. After Trish listened to Janelle's problems at the office, she felt comfortable talking about the nightmare she had been living.

''You have no idea how totally lost I feel.''

''No, I can't imagine,'' Janelle agreed. ''And I feel helpless trying to figure out how I can help.''

''Just be there for me, and be willing to answer all my stupid questions. You must know me as well as anyone.''

She nodded. ''I guess that's true since I joined Atlantis a year before your father died. He loved you dearly. When I heard Andrew call you Trish, it surprised me because your father was the only one I ever heard call you that.''

''Really?'' Trish breathed in wonderment that the one thing she remembered was her father's pet name for her. Somehow his love had remained with her.

''I don't want to prod,'' Janelle said, apologetically. ''But, surely, you've remembered a few other things as well?''

''Like a blue-and-yellow cosmetic bag with butterflies on it?'' Trish asked, looking at her for verification.

Janelle gave her an incredulous look. ''I was with you when you bought it. Why would you remember something trivial like that? It doesn't make sense.''

''None of this makes sense,'' Trish admitted readily. ''I would like to look at a picture of Perry Reynolds.''

Janelle's eyes widened. ''You remember Perry?''

''I'm not sure. When I read his name in the newspaper article, I had a fleeting image of someone. Do you know if I have any photos of him?''

''I imagine so. There are some photo albums in the library. Do you want me to go check?''

Trish nodded, but as Janelle started to leave the room, Trish stopped her. She knew it was childish, but she didn't want to be left alone in this unfamiliar bedroom, trying to become a woman she didn't remember. ''Wait, I'll go with you.''

The library looked more like an office than a place to curl up with a good book. Filing cabinets were lined up against a panelled wall, a large desk held all the components of a computer, and several small stands held copiers, a fax machine and other office equipment. One leather couch and two matching chairs were equipped with study lights as if they were used for nighttime work. Windows looking out on the world were bare except for venetian blinds. Apparently the recent decorator, Eloise, had been forbidden to touch this room.

''Patricia Radcliffe is a workaholic,'' Trish said as if talking about a third person.

Janelle nodded as she stooped down and opened some lower cupboards. ''Even with a partner like

Perry assuming half of the obligations, running a company like Atlantis is a demanding job. It's too bad you were an only child. A couple of brothers or sisters would have lightened the responsibility.''

''Did you know my mother?''

''No, she died when you were a baby. It was just you and your father. Ah, here we are.'' She drew out several albums and some packets of photos that had never been mounted. Glancing at the dates on the outside of the packets, she said, ''It's more likely you'd find one of Perry in these rather than in the albums. I don't think any of the albums are very recent.''

As they sat down on the sofa together, Janelle asked, ''Do you want me to sort through these envelopes and find a photo of Perry, or do you want to look at all of the pictures?''

''Just find one of Perry,'' Trish answered quickly. She wasn't ready to look at the faces of dozens of people she didn't know. She leaned back on the sofa and closed her eyes as Janelle sorted through the photographs.

''Ah, here's a good one.''

Instead of being eager to look at it, Trish found herself hesitating. What if the fleeting image had nothing to do with the name Perry Reynolds? Janelle put the small photo in her hand, and for a moment Trish didn't look at it. Somewhere in the back of her mind, the instant flash she'd had of the good-looking, gray-haired man remained. Very slowly she opened her eyes and looked at the picture.

Her breath caught. Her heartbeat thumped loudly in her own ears.

They were the same. Her instant joy was followed by the stab of a searing question. Why had she remembered him?

Chapter Seven

Trish stared at the picture so long that Janelle must have thought she didn't recognize Perry because she shoved another photo in front of her. "Maybe you remember this one? That's you and Curtis and Perry on his boat. I took the picture when we cruised down to the Florida Keys last fall."

Trish tried to reconcile herself with the happy smiling woman who had her arms linked with the two men's. An air of sexy confidence in her smile was startling. She looked so poised. So sure of herself. Almost daring. Her dark hair was shorter and her face glowed from the touch of the bright sun upon it.

"That's me," she said thoughtfully.

"Of course it's you," Janelle answered in a firm tone as if surprised that Trish might even question it. "And that's Perry and Curtis."

Curtis looked different from the man she'd met earlier. Younger. More athletic. Dressed in white shorts and a yachting shirt. He wasn't looking at the camera but at Trish. Her business partner, Perry, was grinning at the camera and giving a saucy salute with his free hand. A typical vacationing photo, thought Trish. And none of them seemed familiar, not even herself.

"You don't remember the boat or anything about that trip?" Janelle asked, watching Trish's frowning face.

"No. What about Perry's wife? Didn't Darlene go with us?"

"She hates sailing. Gets seasick just looking at the ocean. It's too bad because Perry loves being on the water more than anything."

Trish moistened her dry lips. "It's not true what Darlene was insinuating about Perry and me, is it?"

Janelle hesitated just a fraction of a second before she said quickly, "No, of course not. Darlene is just a young jealous wife who doesn't fit in. I don't know why Perry married her." Then she corrected herself. "Of course I do. Everybody does. His first wife, Dora, was a down-to-earth, plain-looking woman who didn't quite adapt to the social status that came with Perry's financial success. After Dora's death a couple of years ago, along comes sexy, ambitious Darlene, only a few years older than Perry's son, Gary. Well, you can guess the rest. Perry got himself a trophy wife, but pays the price of being married to a jealous woman in the bargain."

"And she thinks he's pulling some kind of trick on her?"

Janelle nodded. "She refuses to have any kind of memorial service for him. According to her, you and Perry have cooked up some scheme to drain all the money and leave her without any."

Trish steadily met Janelle's hazel eyes. "And what do you believe?"

"I think it's a lot of poppycock," she answered readily. "Why on earth would you be faking amnesia?"

"Thank you," Trish said wearily. Trying to convince others that she couldn't remember was an added burden to an already overpowering load.

"You let me handle Darlene," Janelle said, setting the pictures and the album on a side table. Then she frankly eyed Trish. "Is Mr. Davis planning on moving in with you?"

"No, of course, not. I already feel guilty about all the things he's done for me. There's no reason to turn his life upside down, too."

"Then I'll stay here with you for a few days, and run interference. I can be a bear cat when the need arises—at least, that's what the people at the office whisper behind my back." She hesitated. "And when you feel ready to check things out at the company, just let me know."

The thought of facing that kind of demanding inspection in a company of people she didn't remember sent a cold prickling up her spine. She couldn't remember anything about her role as a partner in Atlantis Enterprises. Her expression must have shown her disappointment because Janelle quickly put a reassuring arm around her shoulders.

"It's all right, Patricia—"

"Don't call me, Patricia," Trish said with stiff lips.

"All right," Janelle agreed quickly. "Would you like to see the rest of the house, Trish? And catch up with Sasha?" At Trish's frown, Janelle said, "You hired her as your housekeeper a year ago. She comes in early to fix your breakfast, does the housekeeping chores during the days and leaves after fixing dinner—if you're eating at home," she added, as if that wasn't the usual case. "Don't be afraid to ask her to do anything that will make you feel at home."

Trish nodded, but she didn't know what the housekeeper or anyone else could do to make her feel at "home."

WHEN ANDREW ARRIVED later in the day, Sasha told him that Ms. Radcliffe was resting, but had left instructions that she was to be informed when he arrived.

"Would you like to wait in the small parlor?" the housekeeper asked, her large dark eyes curious as she smiled at him. Obviously, the drama of her mistress's unexpected return had brightened up her routine life, thought Andrew.

"Yes, thank you."

Sasha led him across the hall to a cozy room that was half the size of the living room, and furnished with a stylish upholstered sofa and chairs in a casual decor. He was surprised to see a small spinet piano placed in the corner of the room, and several original watercolors hanging on the wall. It was obvious that someone was a lover of music and art. Trish? He remembered the way she had responded to his efforts with his guitar, and he suddenly felt chagrined at the amateur level of his offerings. Was she an accomplished pianist? Had she spent as much as his yearly salary on one of these original paintings? A bigger question why in heaven had he let himself become emotionally involved? Their lifestyles were worlds apart. He should have handled the whole situation in a sensible, detached way.

Now, she knew who she was, and even if she didn't quite accept it at the moment, she was surrounded with people who would reinforce that identity. When he heard her footsteps in the hall, he was suddenly convinced that the wisest thing for him to do was to withdraw from the whole situation as speedily as possible. This conviction was reinforced when he saw her for the first time as Patricia Radcliffe, wealthy socialite, instead of a drowned waif with fear in her eyes.

Instead of the inexpensive sundress he had bought her, she wore an expensive stylish tunic and pants set in a pale yellow color. Her long hair had been shampooed and swept up in a twist, softened by wispy tendrils falling around her face. She was absolutely stunning. A choked breath caught in Andrew's chest, and he could scarcely breathe.

"What's the matter?" she asked, searching his face. "Why are you looking at me like that?"

"Like what?" he managed, making an effort to get his emotions under control.

"I don't know, like—like you're looking at something you don't like." She smoothed the soft fabric of her narrow pants. "Janelle laid this out for me. She said it was one of my favorites."

"Very nice," Andrew said, forcing a smile. "You have good taste." The minute he said it, he knew he'd said the wrong thing.

"Do I? I guess I'll have to take yours and Janelle's word for it. Nothing in my closet seems the least bit familiar." Her face clouded. His forced reaction had not gone unnoticed. She'd taken the time to look her best for him, and she could tell that he didn't feel any more comfortable with her metamorphosis than she did.

"It'll take time to settle in," Andrew reassured her, realizing he also needed time to get his emotions back on an even keel. All day, he'd been going over what had happened that morning. He had tried to look at each one of the people in her life with as much of a detachment as possible, but he always ended up in the same place. He didn't like Curtis and Darlene, and the jury was still out on Janelle and Gary. "Does anything ring a bell?" he asked.

Trish shook her head. "No. Janelle did her best to orient me, but I felt like someone taking a tour through the place. It's strange, because when I looked over my desk, I understood what the business papers meant, but I don't remember why. I can't put a frame around anything, not even people. And the fear is coming back. I want to run away and hide." She gave a feeble laugh. "Kind of childish, isn't it?"

"Not at all." He reached out and stroked her cheek with a fingertip. "Give yourself some credit."

She stiffened against his touch. More than anything, she wanted to feel his arms around her and hear his soothing voice assuring her all of this was just a nightmare. But she knew better. The time for denial had passed.

"Can we get out of here for a little while?" she said, taking a deep breath. "I really need some space."

"Sure. It's a nice evening. We'll take a walk and find some place for dinner." He was relieved that she hadn't expected him to stay and eat with her and Janelle. Having her all to himself for even a short time was an unexpected blessing.

"I'll tell Sasha." A sparkle came back in her eyes. "Janelle went back to her place to pack a few things. I'm taking her up on her offer to stay around for a few days, and help me get my bearings." She slipped her arm through his. "I warn you, though. You may have trouble persuading me not to run away with you.''

''I'll take my chances.''

THE CLEAR SUMMER evening was one of those cooled by a soft breeze and softened by a glow of myriad stars. As they walked arm in arm under a canopy of trees in Central Park, Andrew wondered how many times Trish had been on these very paths. Surely, living so close, the park was like her front yard.

When she hesitated in front of a fountain and bronze statue, he searched her face. Her eyes had narrowed and her mouth was slightly open in deep concentration.

He started to ask, ''What is it, Trish?'' but caught himself in time. He could see the sudden quickening of her breath, and the rapid movement of her chest.

I remember this place. Recognition of the statue was like a stabbing light coming out of a hidden darkness. She knew that she had stood in that very spot before, and it was the remembered scent of a man's cologne that was the clue to the memory. Her nostrils quivered and for a moment and her fingertips suddenly tingled as if threading the hairs of a man's head. She put her hands over her mouth, but they still felt the bruising of a man's lips. Her emotions were like water tumbling over a fast revolving wheel, spilling and falling in every direction. All of her senses were raw-edged and she couldn't control any of them.

She turned and stared at Andrew until his concerned expression settled the confusion within her. Her mind raced to understand what was happening. Apparently her body remembered things that her intellect refused to acknowledge.

"What it is?" he asked, unable to control himself any longer. "Did you remember something?"

How could she explain that her senses were filled with the embrace and kiss of a man who was a complete blank in her memory? She couldn't remember whose arms had held her, and whose lips had kissed her. Something that Dr. Duboise had said came back to her with frightening validity. *"For some reason, maybe you chose not to remember."*

"It must be true." She looked up at Andrew with pained eyes.

"What must be true?"

"That Perry and I were having an affair. I could tell from Janelle's behavior that she was lying to me when she quickly denied it."

"Is that what you saw? You and Perry?" Andrew knew he shouldn't react to anything she said without thinking it through first, but he couldn't help himself.

"Well, not exactly. I didn't see anything. I just felt it. He must have kissed me right here, and my senses remembered."

"But you didn't actually have an image of Perry standing here with you?" he prodded, and she shook her head. "Then, how do you know it was Perry who kissed you? Surely a young beautiful woman like yourself could have been kissed dozens of times in the park, maybe in this very same spot."

He could have added that for his money, he'd bet on Curtis Mandel. Just the thought put a bad taste in his mouth. Maybe it was jealousy, or something else entirely irrational, but Andrew didn't want it to be either Curtis or Perry. In fact, he didn't want to think about her being in any man's arms. Trying to believe that she'd never felt any man's passion showed how far he'd strayed from reality, he thought grimly.

"Maybe it wasn't Perry," Trish said as if she'd been given a reprieve. She didn't want to think herself guilty of Darlene's accusations. "Maybe everyone just thought we were more than business partners."

"Be careful that you don't let these people put a trip on you," Andrew warned as they started walking again. "Even with the best intentions they could feed you a lot of pure guesses and untruths. Trust yourself and your own feelings, Trish."

As she looked up at him, she wondered how he would react if she admitted that she'd be willing to live with him in his cottage and let the rest of the world be damned? Even as the fantasy crossed her mind, she knew there wasn't any way they could shut out the world for very long.

They finished their walk in silence, and ate at a small Italian restaurant not far from her apartment. Trish lingered over her coffee and dessert as long as possible. She hated to think about going back to her place almost as much as she had been reluctant to return to Havengate. She felt suspended between two worlds—the known and the unknown—and neither of them were to her liking.

"Will you be back in the city tomorrow?" she asked hopefully as they entered the foyer and walked toward the elevators. She had asked Andrew not to come up to the apartment with her because she knew she'd make excuses for him to stay as long as possible.

"I wish I could," he said honestly. "But I have some programs that I have to finish before the end of the week. I've fallen behind on my deadlines and the boss is kinda breathing down my neck."

"I'm sorry," she apologized, knowing that her situation had been a demand on his time. "But I'll miss seeing you."

Her expression made him reach out and put his hands on her shoulders. "Hey, it's going to be all right. Maybe you could drop by the cottage one day after your sessions with Dr. Duboise? That is, if you're not too busy. Things will probably start moving pretty fast once the word is out that you're back. I'm sure there will be some welcome-home parties."

"Parties?" She gulped in horror. Trying to focus on one stranger at a time was excruciating enough. How could she manage a whole roomful of people who would expect her to remember them. "You have to come and be there with me. You will, won't you?"

"Of course," he answered, denying the truth that he hated social gatherings more than anything. He'd never been good at superficial chatter, nor pretending to be enjoying himself when he wasn't. Only the pleading look in her devastating aqua eyes made him willing to suffer a whole evening of that kind of torture.

"Thank you," she said and leaned forward to kiss him on the cheek.

As his hands tightened on her shoulders, he wanted to forget about being the "good guy" and the "trusted friend." A flood of sexual desire fueled a demanding longing to feel the sweet length of her body responding to his. He wanted to kiss her lips, cup her soft breasts and make passionate love to her. As she drew back from her light kiss on his cheek, her smile was tenuous as if she'd sensed his thoughts and was frightened by them.

"I'd better go," she said quickly, not looking at him as she touched the elevator button.

He wanted to say something that would deny his feelings for her, but he kept silent. She had enough to deal with at the moment. Better pretend that nothing had changed.

"You can call me anytime, Trish. You know that," he said in what he hoped was a friendly offer instead of the tense longing of someone falling in love.

She nodded, and as the elevator door swung open, she almost changed her mind and asked Andrew to go up with her. *And then what?* she asked herself. Just postponing the inevitable of being alone wasn't going to change anything. She was being selfish to cling to him like this. How could she expect him to hold her hand at every step of the way? He had his own life to live.

She gave him a casual wave good-night, and watched the elevator door shut him from view. Then she leaned back against the wall, and tried to pretend that she was Patricia Radcliffe coming home to her fashionable apartment. But her fantasy only increased the sickening sensation in her stomach.

When she stood in front of her apartment door, she realized that she didn't have a key. She put an insistent finger on the bell, and was relieved when it only took a moment for Janelle to opened it.

"There you are," she said with a smile. "When I got back from my place, Sasha said you'd gone out to dinner." She peered behind Trish. "Where's Mr. Davis?"

"I left him downstairs."

Janelle's eyebrow lifted almost imperceptibly. "Oh?"

Trish didn't respond to the obvious question, but walked past her into the living room. She saw then that they weren't alone.

Gary Reynolds eased to his feet. "Good evening, Patricia."

"I was trying to get rid of Gary before you got back," Janelle said with brutal honesty. "As you can see, I didn't have much luck."

"I don't mean to butt in," he said quickly, grinning nervously. "I really need to talk with you, Patricia. And if I wait for that stepmother of mine to spew out her poison, you'll never give me a chance to explain."

"Explain what?"

Janelle gave an audible sigh. "I can't believe this, Gary. How can you expect Patricia to bail you out of another mess? We all know your dad put his foot down, and refused to sink any more money into your harebrained schemes."

"Is that what this is about...money?" Trish asked bluntly.

"It's about my inheritance," he said flatly. There was a hardness in his eyes that denied his youth. "Darlene refuses to accept the fact that my father probably took some boat out in the storm and got himself killed. She's holding up everything because she's got this wild belief that you and he are up to some kind of con game."

"That's totally and utterly ridiculous," Janelle snapped.

"I know, but once she gets an idea in that pea brain of hers, she won't let go. She's gathering all kinds of evidence to prevent the authorities from declaring him dead. It's up to you, Patricia, to put them straight."

"Put them straight?"

"Tell them that my father is dead."

Trish shook her head as she dropped down in a chair. She couldn't believe she was having this conversation.

"You idiot, Gary," Janelle snapped. "Don't you have a brain in your head? You know that Patricia is suffering from amnesia. She doesn't even remember what happened to her, let alone your father."

"She knows she almost drowned," Gary retorted, belligerently. "If my father were still alive, he'd have been found by now. Don't you see, if we have to wait for a body to be washed up—if it ever does—no telling how long it will take to settle his estate—and I need the money now."

Trish couldn't believe his callousness. Listening to the spoiled, selfish young man was like sprinkling pepper on her raw nerve ends. She wanted to tell him exactly what she thought of him, and as a number of less than polite adjectives flowed through her mind, she knew one more thing about herself—she could swear like a bawdy sailor if the occasion arose.

Janelle must have been familiar with the look Trish gave Gary, because she said hastily, "You'd better leave now, Gary. You've had your say, and I don't want to pick up the pieces if Patricia loses her temper."

Gary started to protest, but one look at Trish's glare made him change his mind. He swallowed back the words on his tongue, turned on the heels of his expensive loafers and left the apartment, banging the door behind him.

Trish felt strangely elated. From the way Gary and Janelle had reacted, she knew that she wasn't some mealymouthed pushover. Her present state of indecision and confusion was not her normal behavior. Somehow it was reassuring to know that no one wanted to face her temper.

Gary had only been gone a few minutes when the doorbell rang, both Janelle and Trish exchanged exasperated looks. Had he come back to finish the argument?

Janelle answered the door, and when Trish heard her exchange words with someone, she quickly got to her feet, preparing to bolt before anyone else could waylay her.

"Look at what I have!" Janelle said, coming in before Trish could make it out of the room. She was holding a beautiful bouquet of several dozen roses.

Trish's heart quickened with joy. Andrew. He must have stopped and ordered the bouquet before he left the city. She hurried over, took them from Janelle and quickly drew out the white envelope. The smile faded as she read the enclosed card.

> Thinking of you, my darling, and our future together.
>
> All my love,
> Curtis

Chapter Eight

Trish turned away so Janelle couldn't see her face. Dismayed and shaken to the depths, she felt as if someone had just landed a fist in her middle. Even though she had been aware of Curtis's proprietary manner that morning, she had never dreamed that there had been a love relationship between them. In fact, she'd given him little thought, assuming that their connection was a business one. He hadn't even come to mind when she'd had that flickering impression of being in someone's embrace at the park. Her thoughts had been filled with the fear that what they were saying about her and Perry was true.

"Well, now it looks as if you have a new admirer, all right," Janelle said, apparently assuming the flowers had come from Andrew. "He seems like a very nice young man. It's amazing how fate threw you together, isn't it?"

That much was true, anyway, thought Trish, but for some reason she wasn't willing to correct Janelle's assumption that Andrew had sent the flowers. Maybe she was too much of a coward to ask Janelle a lot of questions about Curtis or Perry, she admitted to herself. In any case, she wasn't up to handling another complication that might send her whole life into another downward spin.

''Would you like to have me put these flowers in water for you?'' Janelle asked, burying her face in their sweet fragrance. ''Beautiful. Roses are your favorite flower, aren't they?''

Are they? I don't know. This silent admission seemed to crystallize the utter devastation that went bone-deep. All evening she'd seemed to totter on the edge of remembrance, but even a simple preference for roses as her favorite flower eluded her.

She turned to Janelle. ''I'm very tired,'' she said. ''I think I'll call it a day.''

Janelle nodded. ''I understand. It's been a rough time for you. I wish I knew how to make things easier.''

''You already have,'' Trish said quickly. ''Thank you for being here.''

''Please call me if you need anything. I brought some work from the office, so I'll probably be up until about eleven. I'm in the guest room just across the hall.'' Janelle smiled as she added reassuringly, ''Just a holler away.''

As Trish made ready for bed, she wondered if someone had alerted Janelle to the recurring nightmares she'd been having. No doubt, if she went into one of her crying and screaming jags, she'd scare Janelle out of her wits. It had been bad enough to have Andrew, or the staff at Havengate to help her through those rough moments, but embarrassing herself with Janelle would be worse.

She hadn't wanted to leave the hospital, but Dr. Duboise had been insistent. ''Trish, we don't know how long you will suffer a loss of memory. It could be months, and even years. You're a young, vibrant woman who shouldn't languish in an institution when you could be making a new life for yourself."

A new life. And what do I do with the old one? Trish asked herself as she lay stiffly in her queen-size bed, wearing a fancy nightgown that she would have traded in an instant for Andrew's too-large sweatshirt.

She pictured him lounging in front of the fire, his fair head bent over his guitar, and an appealing softness to his lips as he hummed the melody. Just thinking about the time they'd spent together brought a warmth in her chilled body, but there was a warning there, too. How could she admit to him that every time he touched her, she wanted to forget about the tangled threads of her lost memory and give into a desire that had flared the first time he'd lightly kissed her cheek? If she admitted to the building romantic attraction that she held for him, he might decide to ease out of the picture as quickly as he could.

She had felt an instant gulf between them when he'd first seen her in clothes belonging to Patricia Radcliffe, and she regretted the explosive introduction he'd had to the people in her life. That horrible scene alone must have warned him not to get involved with a woman who had so little in common with his chosen lifestyle. The more Trish knew about herself, the more she realized that the last thing she wanted to do was draw Andrew into a quagmire of her past life. Even though she knew it wasn't fair to Andrew to cling to his support, the thought that he might drop out of her life completely created a sudden sense of overwhelming hopelessness.

It was after midnight when she finally fell into a

restless sleep. As she turned and tossed, a plaguing dream rose from her subconscious to torment her.

She was trapped in a labyrinth of high-trimmed hedges with falcons circling overhead. She cried out as she frantically ran through the maze, trying to escape from their whipping wings and threatening beaks. No matter how hard she tried she couldn't find her way out. Every turn in her path was blocked by someone. Curtis, Perry, Dr. Duboise, Janelle, Gary and Darlene.

"Let me go. Let me go," she begged but none of them would let her pass. Each one of them drove her back into the dark heart of the maze.

She lashed out at them with swinging arms, screaming and gasping for breath.

"Wake up, Patricia! For godsake, wake up!"

Trish jerked awake and sat up, her heart racing and her breath short. Janelle stood over the bed, holding her nose as a stream of blood flowed from it.

"Oh, no," Trish gasped when she realized in horror that in her wild thrashing, she must have struck Janelle when she tried to wake her up.

"You pack a mean punch," Janelle gasped.

"I'm sorry. I'm sorry." Trish slid out of bed and followed Janelle into the bathroom. "I was having a nightmare, and...and..." Her voice trailed off. Janelle wouldn't understand if she tried to explain the dream. How could she? Trish asked herself, when even she didn't understand. Why did she feel persecuted by all these people? She didn't know what was behind the nightmare, but the terror had been real. So real, that even now she felt beads of sweat on her forehead and palms.

As Janelle was bent over the sink, stopping the

nosebleed with soft towels, she kept reassuring Trish that it wasn't her fault. "I got too close. Trying to hold down your arms was a stupid thing to do. I thought I was strong enough, but, girl, you're a wildcat when you're riled up."

They went into the kitchen and put ice on her nose which, Trish saw to her horror, was already slightly swollen. Great, she thought. The one person who has befriended me and I've punched her in the face.

"Don't worry about it," Janelle said, holding a cold compress to her nose. "A bloody nose is no big deal. But I am worried about you, Trish. What kind of a dream could send you into a wild fit like that?"

"I was trapped in a maze and couldn't get out," Trish said, deciding that she wouldn't hurt Janelle's feelings by telling her any more. After all, she might pass along to the others that they, too, had been villains in her nightmare. Not exactly the kind of information that would win any friends under the circumstances. It bothered her that Dr. Duboise had been one of them harassing her, but she was grateful that Andrew hadn't shown up in the nightmare. "I'm truly sorry. I was hoping that maybe I'd get through the night without disturbing you."

"You've had this kind of nightmare before?" At Trish's nod, she looked concerned. "And what does your psychiatrist say about them? Surely he could give you a sleeping pill, or something."

Trish had to smile. Innocent Janelle. No sleeping pill in the world could erase the deep-seated anxiety that tormented her awake and sleeping.

"You're going to tell him about this dream, and see what he thinks, aren't you?" Janelle prodded.

Trish nodded. "I have an appointment with him tomorrow afternoon.'' Then she glanced at her watch. It was two o'clock. ''I mean this afternoon.''

Janelle slipped her arm through Trish's. ''We'd both better catch some sleep or we'll be zombies come morning. I've got to come up with a fascinating story how I got this bump on my nose.''

Trish smiled at her gratefully. She knew that was Janelle's way of saying that they'd keep the whole nightmare saga to themselves.

THE NEXT MORNING, Janelle offered to drive Trish to her doctor's appointment that afternoon, but she said she'd drive herself. She checked a map to make sure she knew how to get to the hospital.

''All right. I'll make arrangements for the attendant to bring your car up for you,'' Janelle volunteered. ''And if you change you mind, just call me at the office.''

Trish took the elevator down to the foyer at the appointed time and was startled to see a white Porsche parked at the entrance. It didn't seem the least familiar and she wanted to ask the young parking attendant if he'd brought the right car, but he tipped his hat, and greeted her with a friendly smile. ''Have a nice day, Ms. Radcliffe.''

She was glad that the valet kept an extra key for each car. There were several personal items in the car like sunglasses and a pair of driving gloves which fit perfectly, but the most startling of all was a beautiful leather briefcase, embossed with her name lying in the front seat. She quickly opened it to see what was inside, but it was empty. Disappointed, she stared at the briefcase as if it could speak to her. When and why had she left it there? None of the possibilities that came to mind made sense.

She left the city behind and took the New Jersey Turnpike to Havengate. At least skills like driving had not been affected by her loss of memory, she realized with relief. Once more she was grateful that the part of her brain that handled learned behaviors remained intact.

She had to wait nearly a half hour for her session with Dr. Duboise, and she found herself getting more and more tense as the minutes passed. She must have communicated her nervousness to Dr. Duboise in her greeting, because he apologized. "I'm sorry about the delay. There was a slight emergency."

He motioned to her usual chair and picked up a file from his desk. "How are things going, Trish?" he asked casually as he took his seat.

Grateful that he hadn't addressed her as Patricia, she answered honestly, "More confused than ever. I don't know if I can even explain what it's like to step into a stranger's life and try to pretend that it's yours."

"Why don't you just talk aloud to yourself about it, and I'll listen?" He leaned back in his chair as if he had all the time in the world.

"All right." She decided not to start with the nightmare because the doctor wouldn't know any of the people in it—except himself. Her hands tightened on the arm of her chair as she told him about her first meeting with Curtis, Janelle, Gary and Darlene. Putting into words what she felt about each one of them was difficult because she wasn't sure herself exactly what her feelings were.

"I like Janelle. She's very supportive and patient with me. As for Curtis, I'd feel rather indifferent about him if it wasn't for the undercurrent of intimacy that he projects. How could I have been in a romantic relationship with this man, and not even recognize it on any level of my being?''

''Do you want to recognize it?''

''What do you mean?''

''Would you like to recognize an intimate relation with him?''

''No, I wouldn't,'' she said without hesitation.

''Why not?''

''He frightens me in a way that I don't understand. He's worried about me, I can tell that.'' She told the doctor about the bouquet of roses and the card. ''I'm not sure but, perhaps, he saw Andrew and me having dinner. Maybe the flowers were his way of letting me know that I'd already made a commitment to him. What do you think?''

As always, he refused to provide an answer. He gave her a reassuring smile and waited for her to go on talking.

Frowning, she tried to describe Darlene and her stepson, Gary. ''Darlene is Perry Reynolds, my business partner's young wife. Gary is her stepson, closer in age to her than was her husband. Darlene made it clear that she believes her husband's disappearance is some kind of a conspiracy between Perry and me to cheat her.'' Trish's mouth quivered. ''She doesn't buy my story about not remembering, and her stepson wants his father declared dead so he can get his inheritance.''

Dr. Duboise leaned forward, keeping a steady eye on Trish's face. ''And you feel caught in the middle.''

''Yes.'' In a halting voice, she told him about the

nightmare. "No matter which way I turned, I was blocked by someone—even you."

"Maybe you're trying to please everyone but yourself," he suggested quietly.

"But I don't trust myself. How can I? I don't know these people or anything that's happened in the past. I want to behave the way I should, but I don't know what's expected of me."

"Do you think it's wise to try and honor a lot of obligations that you don't even remember?"

"How can I be sure I'm doing the right thing unless I depend upon someone else to tell me?"

"You still have feelings, insights and intuition, haven't you? Why not trust them?"

"I'm not sure I can," she said honestly.

"I find you to be a very intelligent, brave person, and I'm confident that you're capable of handling every one of the people you've described to me." He gave a rare chuckle. "And if any of them show up in any more of your dreams, including me, just kick us out!"

She laughed with him and left the session filled with a new confidence that she could handle the next round of challenges. Assuring herself that Andrew had invited her to drop by the cottage after any of her sessions, she didn't bother to call, but headed her car in that direction.

ANDREW WAS JUST COMING up from the beach after a short run when he saw a white Porsche turn off the ocean-side road and head toward the cottage. He wouldn't have noticed the dark blue coupe following a short distance behind if it hadn't suddenly slowed, pulled to the side of the ocean road and stopped in a spot partially hidden by a clump of trees.

Somebody with car trouble, Andrew thought idly, and his interest in it faded when he saw Trish sitting behind the wheel of the expensive car turning in his driveway. As she parked the Porsche beside his weathered old model car, the contrast was a poignant reminder of the difference in their economic status.

She waved and got out of the car when he was still some distance from the house. She watched as his strong legs covered the sandy ground in a graceful stride, his arms moving in rhythm at his side. A mellow afternoon sun turned his suntan to bronze and highlighted the golden cast of his hair. She leaned up against the car, waiting for him with a rush of happiness that defied everything else in her life.

"Pretty fancy wheels," he said pointedly as he reached her, and raised his eyebrows at the white Porsche.

"They say it's mine," she answered with a hesitant smile. "So I decided to believe them."

"Why not? Maybe you own two or three different models to suit your different moods."

She could tell from his tone that the expensive car had already put some distance between them. She suddenly felt uncomfortable. "I hope I haven't come at a bad time."

"Not at all. I couldn't seem to concentrate so I took a jog to clear my mind. I'm glad for the interruption. How did the session with Duboise go?"

She made a noncommittal answer. More than anything, she wanted to shut out all the upheaval of unanswered questions, and just renew herself in the quiet comfort of Andrew's presence. This small cottage was her refuge, and she looked at it with a sense of longing that made no sense at all.

"Would you like to have a drink on the deck?" he asked as if she were polite company.

She heard the reservation in his tone, and didn't know what to do about it. Obviously, he'd had enough of her emotional drama. She knew she should refuse just as politely and leave, but she couldn't.

"Yes, thank you," she answered, matching his formal tone. Preceding him up the steps to the deck, she eased down in one of the patio chairs and crossed her legs. "Something cool would be nice."

He felt the challenge in her manner, and he inwardly smiled. She was a study in feminine loveliness, he thought, eyeing her supple legs and the white silk dress, styled in simple lines of high fashion that molded her slim figure. A delicate gold necklace laced with pearls circled her neck, and matched the tiny earrings framed by her dark shining hair. He couldn't even begin to guess the price tag of this one outfit, but it was definitely a sharp contrast to his cutoff jean shorts and faded cotton shirt. Only the violet shadows under her eyes assured him that she was still the frightened Trish that he'd found on the beach.

As he turned to go inside, his gaze flickered over the beach road and he saw that the parked car was still there. If the driver was out of gas, he'd have about a two-mile walk to the nearest station.

Andrew went into the kitchen and was filling glasses with ice and pouring lemonade into them when Trish joined him. Without an invitation she sat down at the small table, and stared out the window without saying anything.

"Don't you want to go back on the deck?" he asked poised with two glasses in his hand.

She shook her head.

Putting the drinks down on the table, he took a chair opposite her. Thirsty from his run, he took several healthy sips of his drink before he realized hers remained untouched. After a long moment, he said gently, "Do you want to talk about it?"

"No," she said quickly, straightened up and took a sip of her drink. "I've already had my tell-all session for the day. No need to burden you with the ugly details."

"Who said it was a burden?"

She faced him squarely. "You did. Why are you treating me like I'm some distant relative who showed up on your doorstep? I thought we were friends. Last night...last night you made me think that I could come and see you anytime I wanted."

"And you can." He reached to touch her hand but she jerked it away.

"Then why am I feeling that it's some kind of imposition? That I shouldn't be here, taking up your time?" She spoke aggressively because inside she was weak and shaky, and more than anything she didn't want to fall apart in front of him. "I thought that you were the one person who would be honest with me. If you want me to go, just say so."

"I don't want you to go." And to prove it, he pulled her to her feet and folded her into his arms. So much for being sensible, he thought. The bravado of her words hadn't fooled him, and more than ever, he was aware of her vulnerability. "I wish you could stay here."

"Are you sure?" She searched his face as his hands

splayed across her back, holding her firmly against him.

''Yes.'' His voice was thick, and without heeding any of the warnings racing through his mind, he wanted more than anything to show her how much he didn't want her to go. He bent his head and kissed her, not a tender, affectionate kiss but one that threatened to destroy any emotional equilibrium he had hoped to maintain between them. As his questing tongue tasted the sweetness of her lips, and her arching body responded to his, all of his good intentions not to take advantage of her emotional instability were threatened. She returned his kisses with a fierceness that sobered him. With great effort, he drew back, creating a protective distance between them.

''Wow,'' he breathed in a husky voice. ''A burden, you're not. I guess I proved my point.''

''I'm not sure I'm convinced. Would you like to try again?''

She started to put her arms around his neck again, but he laughed as he captured her hands. ''I think that's enough convincing for now. What do you say I change clothes and we go out for a bite to eat.'' He knew he was running scared, but he didn't trust himself to be alone with her for another minute when his hormones were firing like Fourth of July rockets. ''There's a small fish place just up the coast. They have wonderful baked salmon, jumbo shrimp and—''

She chuckled. ''You don't have to give me the whole menu. I understand. You think it's better that we go out.''

''Right.'' He flushed, feeling in some sense like an adolescent worried about coming on to a girl too fast, and in another like a caveman wanting to carry her off to his den. "Yes, it's better that we go out," he echoed, and planted a benign kiss on her hairline before he turned and disappeared into the bedroom.

When he reappeared a few minutes later after a quick shower, he was wearing beige slacks and a yellow shirt that harmonized with the sunbeached hair. Trish wondered how a man could look so damn sexy without even trying.

"Shall we take your car or mine?" Andrew asked.

"Yours," she answered readily.

"I've never driven a Porsche," he said with a little boy's yearning that made Trish laugh.

"Then by all means, let's take the Porsche."

As they turned onto the beach road, Andrew saw that the parked car was still there, and no sign of a driver. If a patrolman saw it sitting there, he'd ticket it for abandonment, Andrew thought, and then dismissed it from his mind.

The small oceanside café was called the Atlantic House, and was built on pilings that reached out into the water. The weathered building had survived countless storms and offered the best seafood in the area.

At first, Andrew was worried that Trish might be uneasy listening to the rippling of the surf and watching the ocean scene just outside the wall of windows, but she didn't seem to pay much attention to her surroundings.

As they dined in the radius of soft candlelight, and listened to the dinner music provided by a small combo, Trish was determined to hold on to a momentary release from a past that she didn't remember, and a future that was as blank as her memory. She found Andrew to be a perfect dinner date. As they sipped glasses of white wine and enjoyed baked fresh lobster tails, their eyes met in a silent communion that shut out everyone else in the room. When Andrew smiled at her, she felt whole and complete, and had the unreal wish that the evening would last forever. Emotionally drained, struggling with the jagged pieces of her life that didn't fit together, the present moment was the only sure thing within her grasp.

As they left the restaurant, Andrew noticed a dark blue coupe in the lot, the same model as the one that had been parked on the road near his house. He would have dismissed it as coincidence if the coupe hadn't appeared a few minutes later trailing behind them on the beach road as he drove slowly back to the cottage.

Keeping his eye on the rearview mirror, he began asking himself if it was the same car that had been parked earlier near his house, and then showed up in the parking lot where they had dinner? There was no doubt about it. A dark blue coupe was keeping a sedate distance behind them, and the hairs on the back of Andrew's neck prickled.

''What's the matter?'' Trish asked, as she watched a tightening of his lips.

''Nothing,'' he lied as his expression hardened.

What in the hell was going on? Why were they being followed?

Chapter Nine

"Why are you suddenly so uptight?" Trish asked, puzzled by the sudden change in his posture. "Is something wrong with the Porsche?"

"No, it's fine." The last thing he wanted to do was put her on edge. He could be wrong about the car behind them. Maybe it was a coincidence.

He deliberately slowed down, inviting the coupe to pass him, but it didn't. Then he sped up, passing several cars, but in less than a minute the same dark blue car was in his back mirror.

"Are you playing some kind of game?" Trish asked puzzled.

"Just getting the feel of the power in this baby," he answered, keeping his tone light. "She's a beauty, all right."

Trish chuckled, pleased that he was enjoying himself. She fell silent, and gave herself up to the momentary peace of just being with him. She had left a message for Janelle that she'd be home late in the evening, and just the thought that Curtis might show up was enough to make her determined not to hurry back.

As they neared the turn off to his cottage, Andrew's

thoughts raced ahead. Would the dark coupe pull into the same parking spot on the beach road? If it did, it was a sure bet that Trish had been followed from Havengate, and that someone had kept them company all evening.

He turned off the paved road, watching in the mirror to see if the blue coupe went by. When it slowed and pulled out on the same overlook as before, quickly dousing its headlights, Andrew knew he'd been right. Someone had been tailing them. Now the question was—what to do about it? Calling the authorities was not an option. The driver of the car hadn't done anything illegal, and putting Trish through that kind of torment would be devastating for her.

As Andrew pulled in beside his own car, he made a decision. Without turning off the engine, he turned in the seat, leaned over and lightly kissed her cheek. "Thanks for a great evening."

His behavior startled Trish. The obvious dismissal was a complete surprise, and his urgency to be out of the car was indisputable. She felt as if he'd found the whole evening too trying and couldn't wait to end it.

She was at once disappointed and a little miffed. "You seem to be in an awful hurry, all of a sudden."

"I've got a lot of work waiting for me," he said, moving quickly away from her, and getting out of the car. "I'd better get at it."

"Well, thanks for dinner. I'm sorry I took up so much of your time," she answered crisply.

"You're going straight home aren't you?" he asked in a rather demanding way as she got into the driver's seat.

She smothered back a sharp retort. Suddenly she was too tired to try and understand his behavior.

Something had gone wrong, but she didn't know what. The roller coaster of emotions that she'd endured since she got up that morning were taking their toll.

"Janelle is expecting me," she told him in a false bright tone. She wasn't going to give him the satisfaction of thinking she'd been expecting to extend their time together—maybe, even stay the night.

"Good night, then." He closed the door, and gave her a wave of his hand as she turned the car around and headed back to the beach road.

He waited for a long minute, just in case she glanced back, before he ducked into the front seat of his own car. Keeping his eye on the Porsche as it turned onto the highway, he waited to see if the blue coupe was going to follow. As soon as he saw it pull out of the overlook, he drove out of his driveway and onto the beach road, following at what he hoped was an inconspicuous distance as Trish drove back into Manhattan.

As Andrew had suspected her tail kept her in sight through all the city traffic, and was behind her when she approached her apartment house. Apparently unaware of the two cars following her, she turned into the underground parking lot and disappeared into the bowels of the building.

"I'll be damned," Andrew swore as the coupe slowed down in front of the building. Andrew kept his gaze fixed on the car, wondering what the driver would do now that the Porsche had disappeared. When it continued slowly on down the street, Andrew followed.

As the traffic thickened, Andrew moved closer and caught a glimpse of a young man at the wheel. He was talking into a cell phone, and didn't seem aware of

Andrew's scrutiny, but in a few blocks, he made a quick left turn, almost leaving Andrew behind.

Sure that he'd been spotted, Andrew sped up, wondering what to do next. The decision was made for him. The blue coupe turned into the parking lot of an all-night convenience store, and the driver got out and headed into the building.

Andrew parked so that he could watch the people traffic in and out of the front doors, and a few minutes later the tall, rangy young man reappeared with a carton of cigarettes under his arm.

As he walked toward the coupe, Andrew quickly got out of the car, covered the distance between the two cars almost in a run, and met the man face-to-face as he prepared to unlock his car.

The man stared at him, and Andrew could tell from his startled expression that the guy recognized him. His eyes widened in his narrow face, and his Adan's apple jumped in his throat as he swallowed hard.

"I think it's time we met, don't you?" Andrew crowded him against the car, prepared to use his fists if the man resisted.

"Hey, take it easy, fellow. No need to get all riled up."

"Then tell me what in the hell you're up to."

"Nothing. Nothing."

Andrew grabbed the collar of his shirt and tightened it around his thin throat. "I want to know why you've been tailing the Porsche."

"Business," he croaked. "Just business."

"Whose business?"

"I can't tell you."

"Maybe I ought to call a cop. I'll file a charge of harassment and then maybe you can tell me."

"All right. All right. You'll cost me my job if you bring in the police." His face was growing red, and Andrew eased up on the choking collar.

"Talk."

"I work for the Decker Detective Agency. And I was on an assignment. That's it."

"Whose your client?"

"I can't tell you that. It's confidential. I could lose my job."

"How long are you going to keep your job if you end up in jail because you've fouled up, and are facing a harassment charge?"

"You can't make that stick," he said belligerently.

"Maybe not, but it won't really matter, will it? Just think about the publicity. Who'd want to hire anyone from your agency to do surveillance? Not a good advertisement if the newspapers get hold of the story. And they will. I'll see to that."

Andrew was surprised at himself. Any kind of macho behavior wasn't his style, but his concern for Trish made him ready for a physical confrontation if necessary. His determination must have been communicated to the young private eye.

The young man's slender shoulders slumped. "All right. It was Mrs. Darlene Reynolds. She thinks that Patricia Radcliffe is meeting her husband on the sly. He's supposed to be missing, but she thinks the whole disappearance is a setup. All I was supposed to do was follow her and see if her husband showed up. I already reported that the only person she met was you. And you don't fit the photo she gave me."

"And that's it?" Andrew was prepared to learn something about the unnamed terror responsible for Trish's nightmares and fear. There was nothing in this situation that related to her pent-up anxiety. She wasn't even aware that she was being followed.

"I can show you my private eye credentials, if you don't believe me." He started fishing in his pocket and drew out his wallet.

Andrew took a quick look at his authorized certification, and nodded. "All right. Just remember I have your name and if you, or anyone from your agency, shows up again I'll have your butt in a sling. Got it?"

"What am I going to tell the boss?"

"That's your problem." Andrew called back over his shoulder as he walked away. "You'll think of something."

Back in his car, Andrew was faced with his own problem of what to do. How could he leave things the way they were with Trish? The memory of her expression when he abruptly ended their evening stabbed him with regret. She deserved to know the truth, that Darlene had hired a private eye to follow her. Besides, Andrew wasn't at all sure that he'd put an end to the woman's harassment. There were plenty of private eyes for hire. As soon as he got home he'd call Trish and explain.

Janelle answered the phone, and when he asked to speak to Trish, there was a slight hesitation. "I believe Patricia has retired for the night."

"She's only been home a short time," Andrew countered. "Would you please tell her that Andrew would like to speak with her?"

"Perhaps you'd better call back tomorrow, Andrew." Janelle's tone was that of an efficient secretary who was used to carrying out the orders of her boss.

"What's going on?" he demanded.

"Nothing's going on. She just doesn't want to talk

to you. I'm sorry, Andrew. I don't know what went on between the two of you but she made it clear that if you called, she didn't want to be disturbed.''

Andrew tried to control his impatience. Obviously Trish was ticked-off about what happened, and seeing the whole thing from her viewpoint, he wasn't surprised. But damn it, he'd like to get the whole thing settled before the rift got any wider between them.

''Why don't you call back tomorrow?'' Janelle suggested briskly.

''Yes, I will. Thank you.'' Andrew hung up the receiver a little more forcefully than Janelle deserved. After all, the woman was just following instructions.

Andrew cursed himself for not having gone to the apartment to talk with Trish face-to-face. No telling what kind of scenarios she was building up in her mind. He'd only been trying to protect her by not letting her know that she was being tailed, and look where it had gotten him.

He was tempted to call Janelle back and tell her the whole story so she could relate it to Trish, but all the things he wanted to say to her shouldn't have to go through a third person. He'd have to wait until tomorrow, and go by the apartment when he was in the office for the day.

TRISH'S INDIGNATION over the way Andrew had treated her had a beneficial effect. It stiffened her resolve to quit holding back from accepting the truth about herself. In her heart she knew that she had been avoiding picking up the strands of Patricia Radcliffe's life because of her romantic feelings for Andrew. Maybe it was childish to tell Janelle that she didn't want to be disturbed if he called, but she desperately needed to strengthen her resolve not to cling to Andrew or the refuge he had provided. It wasn't fair to drag him into the twisted mesh of her life. If he had wanted her to stay and spend the night, she would have accepted the invitation without hesitation. At the very least, they might have shared some intimate moments in front of the fire and shut out the world for a few hours. If only she could have gone on being Trish, none of the miserable things she knew about her life would have touched them. But wishful thinking didn't change anything. She was Patricia Radcliffe with a life to live, and an insidious fear to conquer.

THE NEXT MORNING AT breakfast, she told Janelle, "I want to go to the office with you today."

"Good." Janelle looked surprised and pleased. "You don't have to rush things, though."

"Yes, I do. I don't want to stay in this limbo of not knowing anything. Even if I have to start from square one, I can relearn everything again. Fortunately, my intelligence and command of nonpersonal knowledge has not been affected. And there's always the hope that my memory will come rushing back." She strengthened her resolve. "Then I'll be able to fill in all the blanks."

Janelle patted her shoulder as she got up from the breakfast table. "Okay then. Let's go fight the dragons."

Trish looked over her extensive wardrobe, trying to decide which summer outfit would be the best for running the gauntlet at the office. No doubt people would be lined up to greet her, a little nervous themselves, wondering if it was really true that she didn't remember any of them.

Trish had about decided on a white linen two-piece dress when she saw an opaque garment bag pushed to the back of the closet. Curious, she lifted it down. Then, opening the zipper on the bag and drawing out the contents, she made a discovery that sent the floor rocking beneath her.

A wedding dress! New, beautiful, encrusted with pearls and delicate lace, the garment shouted a designer's original.

In a daze Trish carried it over to the bed, sat down with the exquisite gown spread over her lap. As her fingers touched the beautiful fabric, tears swelled up in her eyes. A deep ache went bone deep. How could she forget something so momentous?

The question was in her eyes as she looked up and saw Janelle standing in the bedroom door. Trish moistened her lips. "It's Curtis, isn't it?"

Janelle nodded, came over and sat down beside Trish.

"What happened?"

"I'm not sure. Everything was all set. I went with you when you brought this dress. It's lovely, isn't it?" she said with a wistful edge to her voice. "The invitations were ordered and everything. Then you changed your mind." There was a slight edge of censure in her voice. "You gave Curtis back his ring, and canceled everything."

"How long ago?"

"A couple of months. He didn't accept your decision then, and he still doesn't. I think he's hoping that all of this will help bring you closer together." She eyed Trish. "Do you think he'll be able to rekindle the romance? Maybe there are some deep feelings left between you."

Trish looked at her blankly. "I don't know the man."

"Not at all? I mean, don't you remember anything about what went on in the office? Outside the office?"

Trish shook her head.

Janelle patted her arm. "Well, don't worry about it, maybe everything will come back today."

TRISH'S VISIT TO THE office was as painful as she had anticipated. Atlantis Enterprises occupied a suite of offices in a Manhattan skyscraper near Central Park. Janelle kept a guiding hand on Trish's arm as they crossed the busy lobby to a bank of elevators.

Trish had decided to wear a two-piece, teal blue dress that was styled in simple but flattering lines. She had twisted her hair into a fashionable roll at the back of her head, and when she checked her appearance in the mirror, she felt that she would, at least, pass inspection in her appearance.

"Our offices are on the thirty-second floor," Janelle told Trish with a reassuring smile as the elevator sped upward. "I've alerted everyone that you're coming, and asked them not to make a fuss. I'll show you your office, and you can take it from there. We want to do whatever makes you comfortable. Whenever you're ready to leave, let me know."

"I'm ready," Trish said wryly.

Janelle laughed as the elevator slowed to a stop at their floor. She wore a light summer suit, and looked every bit the successful career woman. Trish admired her poise and air of self-confidence. *Was I ever that sure of myself?* Trish wondered, trying to still the fluttering in her stomach.

The minute that they pushed through the front glass

doors into the waiting room, it was obvious that Janelle's request not to make a fuss of Trish's appearance had been ignored.

Two attractive receptionists at the outer desk leaped up, and one of them came rushing around the desk to hug Trish. The other woman announced into an intercom, "She's here!"

The next minute the whole secretarial pool was circling around her.

"Welcome back, Ms. Radcliffe."

"Great to see you!"

"We were worried."

Their faces swam in front of Trish like a camera roving over a crowd of strangers. Their bright, friendly expressions were a mockery to the dead feeling she had inside.

As quickly as Janelle could, she maneuvered Trish down the hall. "Your regular secretary is taking some time off for personal reasons," Janelle told Trish. "We have a temp." She nodded at an older woman sitting at a secretarial desk outside a plush office. "Keep everyone out, Agnes," she ordered and swept Trish by her and into the office.

As Janelle closed the door behind them, Trish felt as if she'd run a gauntlet, and for a moment, she just stood there, trying to catch her breath.

"I'm sorry about that," Janelle apologized. "It's just that everyone was ready to go a memorial service, and now here you are, in living color." She searched Trish's face. "Are you all right?"

"I guess that depends upon your definition of all right," Trish answered dryly. How could she explain how totally inadequate she felt to someone as competent as Janelle?

''Does anything seem familiar?'' Janelle prodded. ''Any of the people? This office? The view?''

Trish walked over to a polished executive desk and let her fingers touch the smooth surface. *I've spent hours at this desk and I don't remember even one of them.* Slowly, she sat down in a swivel chair behind the desk, and with a detached sense of a visitor, surveyed the neat placement of everything on it. Instead of touching anything she just folded her sweaty hands on the desk. There was one photograph in a leather frame. Recognizing herself, she stared at a slender, older man standing beside her.

''My father?'' she asked, and Janelle nodded.

She could hear voices in the outer office, and echoing noises from the street below. Looking around the spacious office, she studied the expensive furnishings which she must have chosen. A conversational grouping of a white leather sofa and two chairs were set around a coffee table holding a fresh bouquet of flowers and a silver tea set.

How many cups of tea have I poured sitting there? she wondered.

Janelle had remained silent, waiting for Trish to say something. Both of them jumped when there was a buzz on the intercom. Trish automatically reached for a button, and then froze as a spurt of joy flooded through her. It was a small thing, but she'd remembered. Instinctively she'd responded correctly to the signal. It was the only thing that had happened since her arrival at the office that made her feel she might belong here.

''Yes, Agnes,'' she answered, remembering that Janelle had addressed the secretary by that name.

''I know that you didn't wish to be disturbed,'' the

woman apologized, "but there's a policeman here who insists on seeing you, Ms. Radcliffe."

Janelle moved quickly to the door. "I'll take care of it."

"No," Trish said quickly. "I'll see him."

Janelle looked as if she were going to argue, and then shrugged. "Okay. If you're sure you feel up to it."

Lieutenant O'Donnel was a heavyset man in his early forties. He had receding gray hair, a round face, and glasses, which were perched rather clumsily on his generous nose. There was nothing intimidating about him, and Trish found herself relaxing the minute he introduced himself and held out a soft thick hand for a shake.

"Well, now, it's more than a pleasure to meet you, Ms. Radcliffe. We don't have many missing person cases that end so happily. I just need to ask you a few questions to close up the file."

"Why don't we sit over here?" Trish motioned toward the sofa and chairs, and then gave Janelle a questioning look. "You don't need to stay unless you want to."

"Why don't I just leave the door to my office open in case you need me? My office adjoins yours on one side and Perry's on the other. It's a time-saver not to have to go out into the hall to talk with one another," she explained. "Curtis chose an office at the other end of the hall." She winked at Trish. "He likes his privacy." Then she gave the detective a pointed smile. "I'm sure the lieutenant won't keep you very long your first day back."

"Not long at all." He nodded readily.

Janelle left and the policeman settled down in one

of the leather chairs. "Nice," he said patting the soft arms. "Must have cost a pretty penny."

Trish gave him a noncommittal smile as sat down on the sofa. She also knew he was just trying to set her at ease, but she also knew that his report was going to take her back over the same bewildering circumstances that still had no answers.

He began with routine questions, making sure that the report the hospital had given him was correct. He accepted her state of amnesia as justification for leaving a lot of the form blank. He seemed to just want to get her case off the active list, and she didn't even realize how subtly his questioning began to change. Suddenly they weren't talking about her anymore, but about Perry Reynolds.

She stiffened as he chewed thoughtfully on the end of his pen for a moment. "Let's see, the two of you disappeared at the same time. During the storm, was it?"

"I don't know."

"No, of course not. Sorry about that. We do know he was your partner in this company. I suspect you saw a lot of each other—but, of course, you don't remember that."

The way he said it, the smile on his round face didn't reach his eyes. *He doesn't believe me.* The shock left her momentarily speechless.

"I have a missing person's report on Perry Reynolds filed by his wife." He pulled out another paper from his briefcase. "She says here that she's sure he was meeting you on the day he disappeared—the day that both of you disappeared," he corrected himself. "It's kinda puzzling, isn't it? You show up nearly drowned on a beach, and he doesn't show up at all."

He peered at her, over his glasses, waiting for her response.

She knew then that he wasn't there to fill out a missing person's report. Lieutenant O'Donnel might not even be with that department. His next words verified her suspicions.

"We're looking into Perry Reynolds's disappearance very closely. I don't think Mrs. Reynolds believes her husband is really missing at all. She's making noises like she thinks he's just pulling a disappearing act on her." He peered over the glasses set crookedly on his nose. "What do you think, Ms. Radcliffe?"

He tried to pose it as a friendly question, but Trish knew that it was a baited hook. Her temper flared. "Mrs. Reynolds has already made her suspicions known to me. I didn't have any answers for her, and I don't have any for you." She was pleased with the strong fiber of her reply.

O'Donnel sighed as he replaced the papers. "I reckon we've got a puzzle here, with some of the pieces missing." As he stood up, he thanked her for her time. "Maybe we can have another chat sometime—when you begin to remember things—if you do."

Janelle came through the door so quickly that Trish suspected she'd been listening all the time.

"I don't see how badgering Ms. Radcliffe is going to help anything," she snapped. "You have the hospital reports. Isn't the verification from professionals good enough for you boys? Or don't you understand exactly what amnesia is?"

"Yep, I know. Loss of memory. Sometimes it comes and goes. Kinda convenient like." He gave them a nod of his round head. ''Good day, ladies,'' he said, and left through the door that Janelle was holding open for him.

Curtis was in the outer office as the policeman took his leave. He shot a look at the retreating policeman and then came quickly into Trish's office.

''What in the hell did he want?'' Curtis demanded.

Trish was too sick at heart to answer, but Janelle said curtly, ''Lieutenant O'Donnel doesn't believe she has amnesia. He thinks she knows where Perry is hiding out.''

''Is that true, Trish?'' Curtis asked with questioning eyes.

''What in the hell do you think?'' Trish snapped.

Curtis and Janelle exchanged glances as if to say, ''The old Patricia is back!''

Trish was tempted to walk out of the office right then and there. Only one thing stopped her. Running away was only a solution if you had some place to run to.

Chapter Ten

Curtis walked quickly over to Trish and put his hands on her shoulders. ''Honey, the police put blinders on when they're under pressure to solve a case. Don't give their stupidity another thought. Just take your time. Everything will work out. You wait and see.''

As he smiled at her, she searched his face. Looking into his hazel eyes and following the lines of his jaw and dark hair, there was nothing in her memory to verify that they had ever been friends—let alone lovers. She mentally stiffened. *This stranger was the man she was going to marry.*

She resisted the urge to turn her back on all of them, and admit total defeat. How could she even begin to cope when there were so many unanswered questions? She walked over to the window, staring out at the infinity of tall buildings hemming in the New York skyline.

According to Janelle, Trish had lived all of her life in the city, except for the years she was away at boarding school in upstate New York. This was her home territory. She should have felt comfortable with the cacophony of street noises. Instead, she longed for a quiet beach where the seagulls' wings and the lapping and sucking of the relentless surf were the only sounds to break the hushed silence.

She could hear Curtis and Janelle talking quietly behind her, but with a demanding tumult in her own mind, she didn't even try to overhear what they were saying.

She was startled when Curtis touched her arm. "Honey, Janelle and I agree, you should get out of here. There's no reason to put you under this kind of torture. We can keep things under control until you're ready to take up the reins again."

"It's too soon for you to be loaded down with business problems, especially with all this other pressure that Darlene and the police are putting on you," Janelle agreed.

"We only want what's best for you, Patricia," Curtis told her in his people-management voice.

Patricia. Why did she keep feeling that they were talking about someone else when they used that name? Sighing, she lifted her head and replied, "Yes, I think it would be better to save all of this for another day." *When I feel more like Patricia Radcliffe.*

"There's a nice little French restaurant that is a favorite of yours for lunch." He hesitated as if unsure how to proceed, and searched her face warily. "If you're agreeable, we could go there and maybe talk?"

Her first impulse was to refuse, but she knew that sooner or later the history between them would have to be faced. She'd rather hear the scenario about their relationship from Curtis than secondhand from someone else.

"All right," she agreed. An expression of obvious relief crossed his face, and she realized then how difficult this must be for him. Not only had she broken off plans to marry him, but now she didn't even remember him in the vaguest way. His ego must really be taking a beating, she thought. There was every indication that Curtis Mandel was a man used to getting his way, and for a moment that realization gave her a strange sense of uneasiness.

Janelle beamed. "I think that's a great idea."

"I have a few things to collect from my office, and I'll have to call the restaurant for reservations," said Curtis. "Why don't you come along with me, and see if anything there seems the least bit familiar to you?" The way he asked her gave the impression that she'd spent a good deal of time with him in his office.

"All right," she said, steeling herself for another emotional drain.

As they walked down the hall to his office several people smiled and nodded knowingly as if the two of them being together was a familiar sight. Trish's spirits sank even lower when she saw a picture of herself and Curtis in a gold frame on his desk. They were in evening dress, apparently dancing in a ballroom with a background of glittering decorations behind them.

Following her studied gaze, he said, "That was taken at the Waldorf Astoria, during the company's annual Christmas bash. Perry believed in doing things with expensive finesse. Your ideas were a little less flamboyant. Maybe it's a good thing you don't remember all the arguments you two had about that party every year."

"Was he a hard man to work with?"

"Sometimes," Curtis said shortly and then seemed to catch himself talking negatively about his other boss. "Perry was right on top of things, though. He liked to spend money, but he knew how to make it—for all of us.''

''Do you think Darlene has a right to be suspicious?'' She hated asking the question because she didn't know what part she herself might have played in his disappearance. ''Is there any validity to her accusations that he might be staging all of this?''

Muscles tightened in Curtis's neck cheeks. ''I don't know. I really don't know. It's true that you were really the only one that had his confidence. I can't really believe he'd betray you—unless he had no other choice.''

ANDREW HURRIED THROUGH his morning work with only part of his mind on business, and the rest on Trish. He'd called her apartment earlier and Sasha had told him that she and Janelle had gone to the office.

Glancing at his watch, he saw that it was a little early for lunch, but the Atlantis offices were only a few blocks away, and if he could catch her at lunch, maybe she'd agreed to have a bite to eat with him so they could talk.

As he pushed his way though the throng of people choking the sidewalks, he felt like an adolescent hurrying to see his girlfriend. This driving need to be with someone was new to him. He'd never had anyone get to him the way Trish had. His every thought, dream, and desire was centered on her. He'd spent hours trying to come to terms with a tenuous hope they could overcome all the obstacles between them.

She had to be told about the private eye that Darlene had hired to follow her, but he had to handle it in a way that wouldn't add to her load of insecurity. More than anything, he wanted to let her know that he was there for her, reassuring her that she wasn't alone.

This thought was at the front of his mind as he neared the front of her office building. Then he stopped short right in the middle of the sidewalk. His mouth suddenly went dry as he recognized the couple emerging from the front door.

There was no mistake. Curtis waved down a cruising taxi, and put a guiding hand on Trish's arm as he helped her into the car. Then smiling, he disappeared into the back seat with her. The taxi sped away, leaving Andrew standing alone on the sidewalk.

He swore, turned away and headed back toward his office. He couldn't get the picture of the fashionably dressed, well-to-do Trish and Curtis out of his mind. If there hadn't been such pain in his chest, he would have laughed aloud. What had he been thinking? He should have known that once Patricia Radcliffe found her true self, his homeless refugee would disappear. Only a fool would have believed things would end any differently. For damn sure, he was a slow learner. Once more, he'd experienced the pain of letting his feelings get the better of his common sense.

THE FRENCH RESTAURANT was elegant and exclusive. A soft trickling of a small fountain and lush greenery absorbed the sounds of muffled voices and the efficient service of the staff. A smiling maître d' acknowledged them as regular customers and Trish's stomach tightened as he led them to what he referred to as "their regular table."

Curtis held her chair as she sat down, and then took the chair opposite her. The table was beautifully set with fragile china and glistening silverware. Her traveling gaze flowed over Parisian prints on the wall, the wrought-iron tables and chairs and the embossed menu in her hand. Curtis had said that this was a favorite restaurant of hers. Surely, there would be a flicker of familiarity about something from her past?

She only glanced at the menu, certain that everything was delicious and beautifully prepared, but at the moment the last thing she was interested in was culinary art.

"You order," she said, closing the menu.

"All right," he answered readily. "Would you like your usual?"

"And what would that be?"

He flushed. "I'm sorry. You don't remember what your favorite is, do you? It's sautéed grouper fillet. And you always order a glass of white wine to go with it."

She felt like a child who was being tutored by an adult, and she wished to heaven she'd never agreed to have lunch with him. She distanced herself from the situation, and pretended to look at an ebony statue of a nymph while he gave their order to the waiter.

Last night's dinner with Andrew seemed ages ago. She wondered if Andrew was having lunch somewhere in the city. She wasn't sure whether he was working at home or at the office. He had dismissed her so abruptly last evening, there hadn't been a chance to make any kind of future date. She still smarted from his curt goodbye, but maybe she should have swallowed her pride and taken his call—

"Patricia? Patricia."

Curtis's rather impatient voice broke into her reverie. For a moment the unfamiliar name didn't capture her attention. Then she came to with a start. "Yes, Curtis?"

"I was saying that the best way to handle all this nonsense with Darlene and the police is simply to ignore their ridiculous suspicions. You don't have to put up with that kind of harassment."

"What do you think happened to Perry?" Trish asked him with a directness that surprised her. Everyone else was in a better position to figure out the truth than she was. Maybe it was time she demanded some answers of her own.

Curtis's brow furrowed. "I honestly don't know. Perry seemed preoccupied that last week. I knew he had something on his mind, but I just figured that his wife and son were giving him a hard time. Gary is always needing money to get him out of one scrape or another, and Darlene had insatiable ambitions about keeping up with the upper crust."

"What was my relationship with him?" Trish demanded bluntly.

"I'm not sure." He was silent for a moment, fingering a folded napkin as if trying to decide the best way to say something.

Trish stiffened. Was he going to talk about their broken relationship? She watched his smooth white hands and long fingers smoothing the cloth, and she felt a chill. *Had she experienced those hands caressing her?*

"Are you chilly?" he asked when he saw her shiver. "They always have the air-conditioning set so high that one needs a jacket."

"Yes, they do," she agreed, not wanting to admit that the shiver came from deep down inside her.

Curtis sent a slow penetrating look across her face,

and his deepset eyes narrowed. "You really don't remember me, do you?"

"No. I'm sorry. What little I know about...us is what Janelle has shared with me." *Not only does my mind not remember you, Curtis, but neither does my body. I don't want to rest in your arms, bury my face against your chest, or fill my being with your presence. My heart doesn't quicken the way it does when I'm with Andrew.* Her lips quivered, as she was suddenly filled with an unbearable sense of loss that had nothing to do with her amnesia.

Misunderstanding her visible anguish, he leaned toward her. "It's all right, darling. We'll just take it slow. I want you to know that I haven't changed my mind. Just because you broke our engagement doesn't mean that we can't fix things between us. I admit that I was too possessive and I let our little frictions at the office spill over into our personal lives, but we can change that. Don't you see, all of this may be a blessing. You've forgotten all about our estrangement, and we can put that behind us, can't we, and get back to the way we were."

Trish was slow to answer because she suddenly felt trapped, as though he were deftly maneuvering her into some kind of corner. Certainly, everything he said was reasonable enough, but she didn't like the way it was adding up to a reconciliation from a breakup that she didn't even remember! She wasn't ready for that now—maybe, never.

Fortunately at that moment, the waiter arrived with their food, and she pretended great interest in the beautifully prepared meal set before her. As she picked up her wine goblet, Curtis moved quickly to click his with hers in a toast.

"To us," he said, his hazel eyes deepening as he looked across the table at her. "To the future."

"Whatever that may be," she countered, determined not to be unwittingly sucked into his agenda.

He hesitated as if the toast was not to his liking, then he seemed to recover and gave her a rather thin smile.

An uneasy silence settled on them as they ate their lunch. Trish could feel Curtis's eyes on her throughout the meal, but she gave pointed attention to the delicious food, which was wasted on her lack of appetite. He tried several avenues of conversation but they all fell flat. Obviously the things they had in common required some knowledge of what had gone on before—a knowledge that Trish didn't have.

When the waiter brought the dessert cart to their table, she shook her head. "No, thank you."

Curtis seemed to toy with the idea of having dessert as if determine to command her company as long as possible, but as Trish pointedly ignored him, he asked for the check instead.

As they left the restaurant, he took her arm possessively as if she might run away if he didn't restrain her. They took a taxi back to the office.

She remained in the cab when Curtis got out. "Thank you for lunch. I think I'll go back to the apartment now. Tell Janelle I'll see her later."

"Are you sure you don't want me to go with you? Maybe you shouldn't be alone."

"Why not?"

"You seem a little unsettled. You really should—"

"Would you quit giving me advice, Curtis," she snapped, and then was instantly ashamed of herself. This couldn't be easy on the guy. Obviously he wanted them to get back together, and was doing his best to cope with a sweetheart who didn't even remember him. "I'm sorry, Curtis. I need time to myself."

He nodded, stepped away from the cab and watched as it pulled out into the Manhattan traffic. Trish gave her address, leaned her head back and thought about Andrew. Should she swallow her pride, drive out to his place and be there when he got home? She had his cell phone number. A brief call wouldn't hurt anything. An inner voice mocked her weakness. *Give up, now before you make a complete fool of yourself.*

The taxi deposited her at her apartment, and the smiling doorman offered her a pleasant greeting. As she took the elevator up to her floor, she wondered when she would stop feeling like a stranger trying to make everyone believe that she belonged here. Maybe she didn't. Could there be some horrendous mistake about her true identity? This thought kept plaguing her as she greeted Sasha and then went directly to the library. A Rolodex of names and telephone numbers gave her what she wanted.

She called the number of the doctor listed there. The nurse/receptionist assured her that there was a record file on Patricia Radcliffe.

Trish thanked her and then dialed Dr. Duboise at Havengate.

Apparently orders had been left to put her right through if she called because the doctor immediately came on the line. "Trish. How are things?"

She gave a nervous laugh. "You'll have to wait until tomorrow for the next episode of the Patricia Radcliffe soap opera. Right now, I have something else on my mind. Would you request that Patricia Radcliffe's medical records from her personal physician be sent to you?"

"*Her* physician?" He echoed quietly.

"All right, *my* physician. I want you to check the blood type to see if there's a match, and anything else in the physical records that would provide verification that I am, without question, Patricia Radcliffe. Will you do that?"

"Of course," he answered readily in his usual accepting manner. "And tomorrow you can tell me why you think that's necessary." He paused. "Don't try to handle everything too fast. Give yourself some time."

"Do you think it might be a good idea for me to check back into Havengate for a spell?" she asked hopefully.

He chuckled as if he recognized her urge to run away and hide. "We'll talk about it tomorrow, but, Trish, you can't hide from yourself."

"And that's the problem, Doctor. I don't think I want to be me."

"And you're hoping that there has been some kind of mistake, and you're not Patricia Radcliffe at all, is that it?"

"I guess so. If you want to know the truth, I don't think I like her—me—very much."

"Wait until you have all the evidence before passing judgment. The verdict is still out. See you tomorrow."

Trish hung up the phone and rested her head in her hands. A growing doubt about her identity made her wonder if she was losing her mind as well as her memory.

Chapter Eleven

The next morning Janelle offered to work with Trish in the library so that she might get oriented to the company's computer files. Trish appreciated the offer, and did her best to understand everything that Janelle was explaining about the multilevel operation of the investment branch of Atlantis Enterprises, but very quickly Trish realized that Janelle was moving much too fast and swamping her with details that needed a foundation that she didn't have.

Every question that she asked Janelle only brought another surge of information that had no connection in the nebulous structure of her mind. Janelle could see that Trish was getting frustrated.

"You've had years to learn all this stuff. They tell me that your father used to take you to the office with him when you needed a baby-sitter, and after his death, you practically lived there. If you hadn't taken Perry in as a partner, you probably would have burned yourself out by now. Maybe it's time you loosen the reins a little. Why do you have to push yourself so hard?"

"Because I have a past life that is spinning away from me," she answered, but was relieved when Sasha interrupted them a few minutes later, advising Trish that she had a visitor.

Could it be Andrew? Immediately her heart lurched, and she asked eagerly, "Who is it?"

"Mrs. Reynolds."

Trish groaned, and Janelle made a grimace as she asked, "You want me to get rid of her?"

Trish was tempted to take Janelle up on the offer, but she knew that at the back of her dislike for Darlene was the fear that maybe the woman was right. Maybe there had been something more than business between her and Perry. Could I have been looking for a father figure, and gotten involved with him? she asked herself. Finding the truth might be devastating, but it would free her from the constant burden of guilt about things she didn't even remember.

"I'd better speak with her," Trish said reluctantly. "But if you want to come along for moral support I wouldn't object."

Darlene was standing at the front windows, looking down at the park below when they entered the living room. She wore a silk dress that hugged every line and curve of her shapely body, and her blond hair looked freshly styled. As she turned around, delicate makeup highlighted her pale blue eyes and enhanced lips.

Instead of the accusing attitude she'd displayed earlier, she smiled at Trish and said in an artificially friendly voice. "I hope I'm not interrupting anything. I was going to call but decided to deliver my invitation in person."

Invitation? The word echoed in Trish's mind like a bomb ready to go off. Was there some affair scheduled that she was committed to attend? She shot a quick glance at Janelle whose questioning expression indicated that she didn't know what Darlene was talking about.

"What invitation?" Trish asked, trying to keep the impatience out of her voice.

Darlene kept the artificial smile on her painted lips. "After all you've been through, Patricia, you deserve some kind of a welcome-back celebration. I've arranged everything for an affair at the club. I felt it was the least I could do to show you how grateful we are for your return.

Trish blinked. Incredible! The same woman who had been flinging around all kinds of insinuations about her the last time she was here, now wanted to give her a party. Trish couldn't believe the audacity of the woman, and apparently neither could Janelle.

"You can't be serious, Darlene," Janelle said in disbelief. "Don't you think a memorial for your missing husband would be more appropriate?"

A hard look darkened Darlene's blue eyes. "Men who run out on their families aren't honored with farewell parties. I'm sorry, Patricia, that I accused you of being involved with his despicable disappearing scam. And I want to make it up to you. I've already contacted a lot of your friends and acquaintances and they are delighted to have a chance to celebrate your safe homecoming."

Janelle threw up her hands in disgust. "Did it ever occur to you, Darlene, to run this idea past Patricia before you went ahead and arranged everything?"

"Yes, I thought about it, but I knew that she'd just be shy about having a party in her honor. Don't you see, just being with all her friends might be the thing to help her remember exactly what happened.

Wouldn't it be fantastic if the party brought back her memory?'' The way she emphasized memory made it clear that she doubted very much that Trish had ever lost hers.

So that's it. She's hoping to prove somehow that I'm lying about not remembering anything. She's setting me up.

Instead of being angry about the obvious subterfuge, Trish was strangely challenged. This might be her chance to prove the truth to everyone.

She gave Darlene the same kind of false sweet smile that she'd been receiving and practically cooed, ''I think it's a lovely idea. Thank you so much, Darlene. How thoughtful of you.''

Janelle looked at Trish as if she had to be kidding. Then she shook her head. ''I can't believe this.''

Darlene was obviously delighted with Trish's ready acceptance, and quickly named the time and place.

''Of course, it will be a formal—a black tie affair.''

''Of course,'' Janelle echoed dryly. ''And I just bet you have a new gown you're dying to wear.''

Darlene responded sweetly, ''I always enjoying seeing that nice little velveteen gown of yours, Janelle...if you can still get into it.'' Then she turned to Trish. ''Well, I must run. A hundred things to do. Oh, Patricia, I already talked to Curtis. He'll be honored to be your escort.''

It was Trish's turn to shoot mental daggers at her as she waved a flighty hand. ''Bye-bye.''

When the door shut behind Darlene, Janelle growled. ''I have just one regret, that Perry didn't strangle that woman before he took off.''

''You really think he arranged his disappearance?''

"Knowing he was married to that woman, you have to ask?"

TRISH WAS ON EDGE when she arrived at the clinic for her session with Dr. Duboise later that day. Her steps were quick and her breathing rapid as she approached his office. She felt like someone walking a tightrope.

Her thoughts raced. Had he followed through and compared Patricia Radcliffe's medical records with those that Havengate had made during Trish's stay? What if Duboise had found out they didn't match? Trish realized that it didn't make sense to question what everyone told her—she was Patricia Radcliffe. Obviously, there wasn't any doubt in anybody's mind but hers. Maybe it was pure stubbornness that made her want irrefutable proof. She'd been honest with Dr. Duboise when she told him that being Patricia Radcliffe wasn't a hundred percent to her liking. Was she subconsciously hoping that there had been a mistake because she was running away from something?

As always, Dr. Duboise welcomed her with his easy, relaxed manner. He seemed especially low-key about the session, and gave her the impression that the folder he held in his hand wasn't of much importance. Sitting across from her, he smiled, and asked his usual open-ended question, "How is everything going?"

"I'm not sure." Her eyes went from his placid face to the folder he had laid on his knees. "You tell me. Did you get the medical records?" she asked in a more direct tone than she'd ever shown before.

His eyes held a sparkle of approval as he nodded without comment.

"Well, what did you find out?" Trish demanded

impatiently. "You did compare the physical records, didn't you?"

"Yes, I did," he said, watching her closely. "And what do you think they tell us?"

"That I'm not Patricia Radcliffe?" There was a hopeful edge to the question.

"Is that what you want them to prove?"

Her temper flared. "Just tell me! I want to know. Am I Patricia Radcliffe?"

"Yes."

She stared at him as his answer vibrated in her ears. Her chest suddenly felt as if she'd been clobbered with a ten-pound weight. Trish knew then how desperately she hoped there'd been a mistake about her identity. "There's no question…no chance of a mix-up?"

"None."

She leaned back in the chair, and said frankly, "I was hoping that I was someone else."

"Why?"

"Because I don't like what I'm finding out about her life." She drew in a shaky breath.

"And what are you finding out?"

"I was engaged to marry a man that I don't even want to be around. Just the thought of him touching me is unpleasant. How could that be? Even if I don't remember him, some deeper feelings should still be there."

"Maybe they are."

"I don't understand."

"Maybe what you truly felt for him before is still there, minus all the outward influences that might have confused your true emotions."

"But why would I agree to marry someone that I didn't really have deep feelings for?"

"I don't know what you mean by 'deep.'"

"I don't love him," she said, flatly. "You told me to trust my own feelings, didn't you? Well, I don't think I ever loved him. Apparently I broke off the engagement about a month ago, either because I realized I couldn't go through with the marriage because of my feelings—or something else happened."

"And what do you think that might have been?"

She fell silent. There were too many pressures from all sides for her to speculate clearly about anything that might have happened before, or what was happening to her right now. She thought about the feelings she had for Andrew, and she lowered her eyes, not wanting to expose those feelings to Dr. Duboise.

He seemed to sense her reservation, and asked pointedly, "How about the other people in your life? Are you experiencing a little ambivalence toward them, too?"

Trish gave a short laugh. "A little ambivalence? That's putting it mildly."

She told him about her unproductive trip to the office, the uncomfortable session with Lieutenant O'Donnel, and Darlene's plans for a welcome home celebration.

"It's obvious that the police don't believe me when I say I know nothing about Perry's disappearance. I'm not sure they even believe I have amnesia." She gave him a wry smile. "They must think I'm pretty clever to fool you and everyone else at Havengate."

"We've had a visit from the authorities," Dr. Duboise admitted. When Trish's eyes widened, he assured her, "We will maintain patient-doctor confidentiality even if there's an official investigation."

"I know Darlene is convinced that I'm lying,"

Trish told him, trying to control her dislike of the woman. "This party she is giving is just a ploy of some kind. I can't think of anything I'd rather not do than spend the evening trying to pretend I know a bunch of people who are strangers to me. I agreed to go because I'm sure she's attempting to trip me up, and I want to prove to everyone that I am not playing games."

Suddenly her eyes filled with tears as feelings of frustration and despair washed over her. "Maybe it is really true that I don't want to remember."

"That's possible," he agreed quietly.

"Maybe what they suspect about Perry and me is true," she said in a choked voice.

"And maybe it isn't. Why not accept your own intuition, instead of believing what other people are telling you?" He gave her a reassuring smile. "Refuse to let anyone or anything take away a deep confidence in yourself."

"I'll try."

She left his office filled with a new determination to depend upon herself as much as was humanly possible even when she had no idea how the pieces of her life fit together. As she made her way to her car, she had a flicker of regret that she had to go back to her fancy high-rise apartment instead of staying at the clinic.

She was just about to get in the car when she sensed movement behind her. She swung around, startled until she saw who it was.

"Andrew," she gasped, leaning back against the Porsche in relief.

"I'm sorry. I didn't mean to frighten you," he apologized quickly. "I've been waiting, hoping to catch a chance to talk with you."

She was surprised at the sudden quiver of joy that raced through her just seeing him again. Her breath was short and it was only with great effort that she managed to feign an air of indifference. "What's on your mind?"

"I think we need to talk. Could we take a short walk through the grounds before you head back to the city?"

"I'm in no hurry," she admitted. His manner was slightly stiff, and certainly lacking the easy companionship they had once enjoyed. Her initial impression that he was there to invite her to come back to his cottage instantly faded.

Even though Andrew didn't touch her, he was conscious of her nearness as they left the parking lot and followed a stone path circling through the landscaped grounds. He had rehearsed a dozen times in his mind what he wanted to say to her, but his mind was as muddled as ever. Should he say something about seeing her yesterday? Would she think he was spying on her if he admitted he saw her getting into a cab with Curtis?

As he glanced at her, he could see a tightness in her mouth, and faint worry lines fanning away from her eyes. More than anything, he wanted to draw her into his arms and kiss away the traces of tears on her cheeks. Her session with Dr. Duboise must have been a rough one.

He gave her a self-conscious smile, and asked, "How are you doing?"

"Okay," she lied. Maybe if she didn't unload on him, he wouldn't cut her off the way he had the last time they were together. More than anything, she wanted to savor Andrew's company if only for a little while. He was the only one who made her feel that she could be herself even if she wasn't sure just who that was.

"How about you?" she asked politely. "Is your work going well?"

He started to make some superficial response but something stopped him. The truth was that he hadn't been able to put in a decent hour's work since she'd refused his telephone call. He'd spent hours running on the beach, trying to wear himself out so he wouldn't think about her being with Curtis Mandel and all her fancy friends.

When they reached the familiar bench where they had sat and talked before, he eased her down beside him. For a long moment, they just sat there in silence, keeping a few inches between them as if it were crucial to maintain some kind of safety zone.

Trish wondered if he could hear the wild beating of her heart, or sense the desire to turn and bury her face in the inviting strength of his shoulder.

"Trish, I need to get something off my chest," he finally said, clearing a hoarseness in his voice. "I know that you don't need me complicating your life, but I want to explain a few things to you."

"You don't have to explain anything," she said with a lift of her chin. "What happens to me now isn't your responsibility."

"It's not that. It's about the other night."

"I don't blame you a bit for wanting to put some distance between us," she told him as evenly as she could.

"That isn't true." His eyes searched her face. "You think I intended to end the evening that way?"

"The fast peddling you did after our dinner date was clear enough. I got the message, loud and clear."

"I don't believe this." His expression was one of total dismay. "Is that why you refused my call? You thought I was giving you the brush-off?"

"Yes. It was quite obvious."

Relieved laughter came from deep within his chest. "That's rich."

"What's so amusing?"

"My sweet Trish, I thought you were doing the same to me by refusing to speak with me when I called. It seems we both jumped to the wrong conclusions."

"But I don't understand. Why did you behave the way you did?"

"Let me explain." He told her about the car that had tailed her, and the reason he had hurried her away from his place so he could follow it. When he told her that Darlene had hired a private detective to follow her, Trish's mouth literally dropped open.

"I can't believe it," she gasped.

"It's true." He took her hand. "I'm sorry you have to put up with this kind of harassment. She's obviously venting her frustrations on you. The P.I. said he was supposed to report any contact you had with her missing husband. Apparently she's convinced he's hiding out somewhere, and you know where he is."

Trish said wearily, "You'll never guess what she's got planned now. She's throwing a big bash at some fancy club for me as a welcome-home celebration. What she hopes to prove is beyond me. I know she doesn't believe I have amnesia—but neither do the police."

"What?"

Trish told him about Lieutenant O'Donnel's visit to her office, and his obvious interest in her relationship with Perry. "Dr. Duboise told me the authorities have even made inquiries at Havengate about me." Her lips quivered. "I guess Darlene has convinced the police that my disappearance is tied up with her husband's, and doesn't believe for one minute that I've lost my memory."

"Are you going to attend her party?" Andrew asked. "I wouldn't trust her for a minute. No telling what she has planned."

Trish nodded. "I was thinking the same thing. Obviously, she wants to prove that my amnesia is false, but whatever scheme she has concocted will backfire, and prove to everyone that I'm telling the truth."

"Maybe," he said, without much conviction. "But are you up to that kind of trial by fire?"

"I'm not sure," Trish admitted. Just the thought of spending an evening in that kind of war zone would demand all the determination and strength she could muster. "I'm not sure I can do it."

"If that's what you decide you want to do, you'll see it through. I have no doubts that you can put Darlene in her place with great finesse."

"Do you really think so?"

"I do." He touched a strand of hair dangling over her cheek, and gently eased it back behind her ear. His eyes traced the beautiful line of chin and neck. A perfect cameo, he thought. This image of her beautiful face was one he wanted to savor, and draw upon in the lonely times ahead of him.

"I'll need an escort, of course," she said boldly. When he didn't answer, she asked, "Did you hear me? I'll need someone to go with me."

He pulled back from the reverie of capturing her beauty deep in his mind. "What?"

"I said I'll need an escort for the party."

"I'm sure you won't have to look far for one," he responded as casually as he could. Just thinking about her and Curtis paired up at the affair brought a tightening in his stomach.

"No, I suppose not," she agreed saucily. "In fact, I could find one as close as this. Right under my nose." She put her face a tantalizingly inch away from his. "Couldn't I?"

Andrew didn't bother answering, but claimed her mouth in a kiss that momentarily put an end to the discussion. The only reality of the moment was the sensation of exploding warmth and desire that shot through him as he folded her into his arms. It didn't matter that they were visible to anyone strolling through the grounds. It didn't matter that his pain would be heightened by giving in to an impossible longing. Nothing mattered except that for the moment she was his to kiss and caress. As they clung to each other, his lips trailed light kisses from her mouth, along her cheek, and to the warm crevice of her neck.

Trish let the urgency of his passionate kisses sweep her into a mindless state. From deep within, she drew on the assurance that this explosive passion was true and right for her. She almost felt a sense of resentment and betrayal when he abruptly withdrew from their embrace, and firmly set her away from him.

"No," he said in a hoarse voice. "This isn't fair."

She fought for breath and composure. His sudden

withdrawal was like that of a Ferris wheel dropping out from under her. She didn't even know what he was talking about.

“Fair?” she repeated, frowning in confusion. “What isn't fair?”

“Taking advantage of you like this.” His gaze caressed her face. “God knows, I want to forget about everything but making love to you. You have no idea how just thinking about you destroys all my thoughts of bcing thc good guy. It's damn hard to maintain my integrity in this situation.”

“I don't understand. We're both adults. Unmarried…?” She made the word a question. “You aren't married, are you?”

“No. Not now, not ever.”

“Then…?”

He pulled her to her feet. “Let's walk. I can think better when you're not sabotaging my every thought and when your nearness isn't sparking a fire of lustful thoughts.”

Trish was confused. He didn't even take her hand as they began walking back toward the parking lot. She couldn't understand why he was talking about integrity when her passion was raging as fiercely as his. She forced herself to remain as calm as her emotional equilibrium would allow. “Just how are you taking advantage of me?” she asked in a conversational tone. “As far as I know I'm in a position to make my own decisions.”

“Are you?” he asked quietly.

The simple question vibrated between them with the force of a cannonball. In those two words he had landed a bull's-eye. He was questioning her ability to make decisions in a vacuum devoid of past experiences and knowledge. He had every right to be cautious about entering a relationship with someone who couldn't even seem to relate to her real name.

Even though she was convinced that what she felt for Andrew would withstand any challenges of her unknown past, she realized it wasn't fair to expect him to feel the same way.

She forced a smile. "You're right, of course. Even though I'm perfectly willing for you to take advantage of me in any way you choose, I accept your reluctance to go any farther with an intimacy between us. I shouldn't involve you in the tangled mesh of my past and present."

He stopped walking.

"Wait a minute." He put his hands firmly on her shoulders, and looked directly into her eyes. "It's not *me* that we're talking about, but *you.*"

"What about me?"

"How could anyone in your position really know what their true feelings are? I'd willingly carry you off to my lair, the world be damned, but you're in a vulnerable place now. Taking advantage of your state of mind, and emotional upheaval is something I can't do. Do you understand?"

She wanted to say no, but his sincerity and integrity wouldn't let her. In her heart she knew that the time wasn't right for any kind of commitment from either one of them.

"I do understand," she admitted. "But I don't like it." She suspected that most of the reluctance was on his side and couldn't help but say so.

"God knows, I'd be willing to do anything for you."

"Like escorting me to Darlene's party?"

He saw the twinkle in her eye, and knew he'd been deftly backed into a corner. "What about Curtis?"

"What about him?"

"It would be my guess that he expects to take you," he said casually as they reached her car.

"Maybe," she said, knowing fully well that Andrew was right. "But I'm taking you." She didn't look forward to informing Curtis or Janelle who her escort was going to be, but having Andrew at her side was going to be a lifesaver. She deliberately put her arms around his neck, and gave him a kiss that promised much more than a friendly goodbye.

He suspected that if he asked her to come with him to the cottage, she would have readily accepted. Her eyes were hazy as he withdrew her arms and opened the car door for her. If she didn't leave now, his willpower was going to reach a dangerous low.

"I'll see you Saturday night," she said as she slid into the front seat. "Oh, by the way, the affair is formal."

"My jogging sweats won't do?"

She laughed, knowing full well that he'd wear a tux with the same natural masculine grace he displayed in any casual attire. She was almost looking forward to the evening, and tried to ignore a quiver of intuition warning her that Darlene would do her darnedest to embarrass her any way she could.

Chapter Twelve

Trish looked carefully through the array of expensive gowns hanging in the walk-in closet and found nothing that appealed to her. Most of the evening dresses were tight, low cut and loaded with sequins or beads. At the edge of her mind was the urge to find something that would please Andrew. Because he was so laid back about his own attire she knew his tastes didn't run to the flamboyant and conspicuous. In any case, she certainly didn't want to set herself up to be the center of attention any more than was necessary.

Janelle listened to Trish complaining that she couldn't find anything to wear, and laughingly replied, "Well, then I guess a shopping trip is in order."

Trish hesitated, afraid that the outing would prove to be another frustrating and uncomfortable experience, but she didn't see any way around it. She wanted her first time out in public with Andrew to go as well as possible under the bizarre circumstances.

When she and Janelle entered The House of Cherie on Fifth Avenue, there could no doubt about the fact that Patricia Radcliffe was a favorite customer. Madame Cherie greeted her with so much ceremony that Trish was embarrassed. She was grateful that Janelle managed to staunch the woman's exuberance enough to maneuver them into a private fitting room. A younger, less demonstrative saleslady, Ms. Adele, was waiting to serve them, but it took more than an hour before the message finally got through to Ms. Adele that Trish wasn't interested in designer names or original gowns.

Obviously disappointed, the saleslady finally listened to Trish and began bringing out some less dramatic styles.

"I like this one," Trish said finally with a sigh of relief as she selected a dusty-rose silk gown fashioned with a simple bodice that modestly showed off her neck and shoulders. A draped skirt flowed with her as she walked, and her dark hair glistened beautifully against the soft pastel fabric.

Janelle seemed surprised at her choice but nodded approvingly as Trish modeled it for her.

"Do you think Andrew will like it?" Trish asked impulsively.

Janelle's eyes rounded. "Andrew?"

"Yes." Trish smiled happily. "He's agreed to be my escort."

"But...what about Curtis? I mean, everyone will expect you to go with him. You two are a—a couple," she stammered.

"I thought you said that I broke off the engagement a month ago."

"Yes, but after all that's happened, Trish, I know he's willing to start anew and dismiss all the unpleasantness that you can't even remember."

"Maybe I do remember—"

"What?" Janelle gasped. "Is your memory coming back?"

Trish shook her head. ''Not really, but I have gut feelings about things and I know that whatever was between me and Curtis is over.''

''And what about Andrew Davis?''

''I don't know,'' Trish said thoughtfully. ''We'll have to see how things go.''

ANDREW WAS THINKING along the same lines as he left the rental store with a tuxedo box tucked under his arm. He had no idea what he'd let himself in for. The whole evening could be a fiasco. He must be some kind of lovesick fool to even agree to go. The affair was going to be held at a fancy club on Long Island, and it was a sure bet that he would feel about as comfortable as a clown at a royal wedding. Only the thought of spending the evening at Trish's side made the whole thing palatable. He was confident he could handle himself in the elite company, but some inner voice mocked him with possible complications over which he'd have no control. What if Curtis or another of her fancy friends whisked her away the moment they arrived? A beautiful woman like Trish must have a whole chorus of men after her. And what if she became so involved with other socialites that she forgot even he existed? The more Andrew thought about the whole affair, the deeper went the conviction that it had been pure stupidity that had made him agree to be Trish's escort.

WHEN THE NIGHT OF THE party came around, he was still filled with reservations as he arrived at her apartment, a floral box in his hand, and a forced smile on his lips. As he waited for someone to answer the door, he was as nervous as an adolescent calling on his prom date.

"Oh, come in, Mr. Davis," Sasha greeted him with a look that traveled from his blond head, down the length of his tux to his polished black shoes. Then she gave him an approving wink, and ushered him into the living room. "I'll tell Miss Patricia you're here."

The housekeeper knocked on Trish's bedroom door, and told her that Andrew had arrived.

Trish was as nervous as Andrew when she entered the living room, and both of them stood there looking at each other. She had expected him to look handsome in evening clothes, which he certainly did. And she'd been prepared for her heart to quicken in his presence, which it also did. What she wasn't prepared for was the rush of hot passion that was more wanton than ladylike. She flushed as sexual desire sent a hot hunger through her. She would have much rather invited him into her bedroom than do anything else at the moment.

Andrew saw the flush rise in her face and wondered what was wrong. Was she embarrassed by the way he looked? Had he committed some kind of social faux pas without even knowing it?

"Is something wrong?" he asked. "You did say it was formal, didn't you?"

"Yes, the tuxedo is perfect," she hastened to assure him, trying to restrain the urge to put her hands on him.

"Well, that's a relief. I thought for a minute that I'd goofed."

"Not at all. You're perfect."

"And so are you." His own breath was as heavy as hers as his gaze drew in her loveliness. Her lustrous dark hair fell in a soft waves to her shoulders, making a perfect contrast to her fair skin and the gown's delicate rose color. A simple strand of pearls and matching tiny earrings were her only jewelry. She looked elegant and yet utterly unpretentious. Certainly, there was nothing about her that resembled the shivering, disheveled foundling that he'd rescued from the beach. He couldn't believe that this devastating woman was looking at him with such soft, loving eyes.

He stood there, mesmerized by her loveliness, forgetting that he was holding the florist box in his hand.

She smiled and nodded. "Is that for me?"

He came to with a jolt. "Sorry. As you can tell I'm not really hep with this kind of thing. I chose roses because they seemed to be the safest bet." He didn't tell her that he'd almost bought an orchid, but decided that might be too ostentatious. He wasn't even sure a corsage was in order.

"Pink rosebuds are perfect," she assured him as she took them out of the box. Then she handed him the flowers and the corsage pin, and stood so close to him that she could smell the spicy tonic of his clean-shaven face.

He was surprised that his hands were steady and sure as he fastened the flowers to the bodice of her gown. He hoped she couldn't tell that he was fighting the urge to draw her into his arms and crush the flowers in a fierce embrace. With the slightest encouragement he would have scuttled the whole darn evening. He knew then what a challenge it was going to be to share her with anyone else even for a brief time.

"I suppose we have to go," she said softly as if reading his thoughts.

Even though he was tempted to sabotage the welcome back party, he knew that it just might be the impetus for bringing back her memory. He couldn't be responsible for holding back her recovery.

"Yes, we have to go," he said firmly, as much for himself as for her.

As they started down in the elevator to the lobby, he wondered if they were taking his car. Surely, she would rather arrive at the club in her Porsche. "Are we taking your car?"

"Darlene said she was sending a limo."

As they stepped out into the foyer, they met a glowering Curtis face-to-face. Andrew instantly stiffened and shot a questioning glance at Trish.

"I think Janelle is about ready," she said, giving Curtis a lukewarm smile. "It's nice of you to escort her."

"Oh, I'm Mr. Nice Guy," he said with gravel in his voice. His cutting glance at Andrew spoke volumes. "I don't see why Darlene had to send two limos. Surely the four of us could have managed in one."

Trish just shrugged. She could feel Curtis's eyes biting into her back as they walked out of the building.

Two black limousines were lined up at the curb. A uniformed driver quickly opened the door of the first one, nodding and smiling at them.

Andrew followed Trish into the car, feeling like someone who was there under false pretenses. He'd only been in a chauffeur-driven limousine once before when one of the executives of his company had given a holiday party at his estate and some of his coworkers had shared the cost of arriving in style.

As they drove through Manhattan and headed toward Long Island, Trish could tell that Andrew wasn't feeling comfortable in this situation. Where was the friendly companionship they had experienced with each other? She feared that the closer she came to finding the real Patricia Radcliffe, the greater the distance would be between them. He already had his guard up against any kind of commitment to a future relationship.

Instead of sitting close to her in the limo, he had left a respectable space between them as if he either didn't trust himself, or was worried about what the driver might think if he looked back and saw them in an embrace.

She adjusted the lacy shawl she had around her shoulders, more chilled by his remoteness than by the night air. A sense of defeat settled on her. Any attempt at conversation between them was stilted and soon died. By the time they reached the fashionable private club spread out along the water, they emerged from the limo like two people escaping from a stifling situation.

Even before they had taken a dozen steps Trish and Andrew were surrounded by guests emerging from cars that were also being parked by valets.

"Patricia, darling, how wonderful to see you."

"We were devastated, thinking the worst had happened."

"But here you are. Looking absolutely divine."

"Is it really true? You don't remember anything?"

Trish's rising panic was communicated to Andrew as her steps faltered, and he felt the muscles of her body stiffen as if ready for flight. Slipping his arm around her waist, he held her firmly against his side as they moved through the gawking crowd into the building.

The large ballroom was brightly lit with shimmering

crystal chandeliers. Beautifully set tables surrounded a center dance floor, and a group of musicians occupied a raised platform at the far end of the room.

Darlene squealed with artificial joy when she saw them. She was wearing a strapless, shimmering fuchsia gown that barely covered her full breasts. An array of diamond jewelry flashing on her neck, hands and arms was almost blinding.

"Everyone has been asking about you," she bubbled. "Your table is right in front, so everyone can see how wonderful you look." She gave Andrew a quick once-over and then smiled as if he'd passed inspection. "I've been telling everyone that Patricia was coming with her very own hero, the gallant man who had rescued her." She gave Trish a playful shake of her finger. "And you can't keep him all to yourself. You have to share."

Andrew tried not to grimace. He'd only been there less than five minutes and he already felt nauseated. Trish looked a little green herself as he held out her chair and they sat down at a round table, center stage, at the edge of the dance floor. Fortunately there were only two chairs at the small table, but people at the other nearby tables were close enough to make a conversational gathering of a dozen or more.

Darlene kept dragging people over to their table. "Surely you remember Beverly Phillips. You went skiing with her in Colorado last winter."

The young woman had a round face, slightly freckled nose and short carrot-red hair. Trish searched every feature for some mental quiver of recognition. Nothing.

Trish hated the disappointed look on Beverly's face when she said, "I'm sorry. I truly am."

Tears welled up in the young woman's round eyes. Impulsively, she hugged Trish. "Oh, Patricia. I'm the one who's sorry," she said and then hurried away, gently wiping at her eyes.

Darlene walked away with obvious irritation, and Andrew saw her vigorously talking to someone as she nodded toward their table. Just as he had expected, she was going to keep the pressure on Trish, hoping to show that her amnesia was just a sham.

When other partygoers continued to push themselves at Trish, apparently in the hopes that they would be the ones she would remember, Andrew wondered if Darlene had created some kind of a weird lottery. Even the kindest, most polite friends couldn't seem to resist the "remember when" questions.

"Surely you remember the fun we had in Las Vegas last year?"

"What about the time we all went skiing in the Rockies, and you decided to try..."

On and on they went as if recounting every detail would suddenly make Trish jump up and say joyfully, "I remember everything. Thank you, thank you!"

They had only been at their table a short time and had ordered drinks when Andrew realized the only private place was going to be the dance floor.

He stood up, offered his hand and said politely, "May I have this dance, Ms. Radcliffe?"

Giving him a grateful smile, she went into his arms, and he deftly guided their steps into the center of a crowd of dancers. Closing her eyes, she let her cheek rest against his. In the cradle of his arms, she nestled against the graceful length of his body with quiet ease. The nightmare surrounding her dissolved into a momentary peace. She was delighted to find that he was a relaxed dancer, moving gracefully and guiding her with a gentle touch. His love of music was evident in his natural rhythm. They didn't speak, but let the harmonious movement of their bodies communicate the rising awareness of each other, and a suspended detachment from the gawking crowd around them.

When the song ended, they lingered on the dance floor, and ignoring speculative glances coming their way, they enjoyed several more dances before reluctantly making their way back to the table.

They had just seated themselves when Darlene's stepson, Gary approached them with a pugnacious set to his chin. His scowl spoiled his young good looks. He put his hands on the table and leaning toward Trish, he demanded, "Aren't you getting tired of your little game, Patricia? You know exactly what happened. Someone ought to wring the truth out of you. My father's dead and you're too chicken to admit it."

Trish was too taken back by the force of his malevolent behavior to find any words to respond. She couldn't believe that she'd become a pawn in this destructive tug-of-war. Perry's wife was doing everything she could to force Trish to admit he was alive, and his son was beside himself wanting Trish to confirm that his father was dead. She suddenly felt sick to her stomach. *Did Gary already know his father was dead because he had a part in it? Maybe she didn't want to remember the truth of what had really happened to Perry?*

"Gary, watch your mouth before I shut it for you," Andrew threatened.

"Get in line," Gary snapped, looking like someone on the edge of a precipice, being forced to jump.

At that moment, Curtis and Janelle approached the

table, and Gary glared at them with fiery anger. Without even a nod, he deliberately turned his back on them and stalked away.

"What's the matter with him?" Janelle asked, raising her eyebrows.

Trish just shook her head, painfully aware of curious glances coming from people seated at nearby tables. The buzz of conversation all around them verified that Gary's outburst had been overheard. She wanted to sink out of sight, right then and there.

"He's just being Gary," she managed to say with a false smile.

"Would you like for me to have a talk with him, Patricia?" Curtis asked in his take-charge manner. "You don't have to put up with any kind of harassment from him. He's a spoiled brat and everybody knows it."

"Just let it go, Curtis," Trish answered with a stern look at him. What she didn't need at the moment was some self-appointed Galahad creating a bigger scene.

Janelle said smoothly, "I was about to slip away to the ladies' room. Would you like to join me, Patricia?"

"Yes," Trish answered readily with a grateful look. As they left, she glanced at Andrew and Curtis, standing beside the table. She wondered if Curtis would stay and talk with Andrew or pointedly return to his table.

As it happened, Andrew was wondering the same thing and decided to force the issue. "Sit down, Curtis. You know how these women are. We could be left hanging for a while."

"Very well," Curtis answered stiffly. "We might as well take advantage of their absence and have a frank discussion. I'm not sure you understand how detrimental your continuing presence is to Patricia's recovery.''

Andrew kept his expression neutral. ''Detrimental?''

Curtis nodded, sat down and focused his hard gaze on Andrew. ''You must realize that the sooner Patricia is able to function normally in all areas of her life, the greater the chance she has to recover her memory or to move forward in her life in her present state. Holding on to her confusion only delays the inevitable.''

''And what is the inevitable?''

''Accepting the truth about herself and the fulfilling life she deserves.''

Andrew nodded. ''I agree with that completely.''

Curtis's expression hardened. ''Then why are you trying to capitalize on ill-fated circumstances for your own selfish benefit? You know as well as I do that Patricia only wants your company because she's confused. If it's money you're after, I'm sure we can come to some acceptable arrangement. I've checked into your background, and it's obvious that you see this relationship with Patricia as a golden opportunity to make up for the obvious depravation of your past life.''

Andrew smiled. ''I've done a little investigating myself, Curtis. You were a lowly clerk in several investment firms before joining Atlantis Enterprises. You've always had richer tastes than your income and it wasn't until Perry Reynolds moved you into the top strata of the company, and you began dating Patricia Radcliffe that you had money to live in the style you thought you deserved. Let me ask you a question. Is there anything you wouldn't do to ensure your present lucrative position? Even marrying Patricia to keep it?''

Curtis's expression hardened with instant fury. ''My relationship with her is none of your damn business. And you'd better remember it!'' His hands clenched as if he wanted to put them around Andrew's neck.

''Are you threatening me?'' Andrew asked coldly.

''Take the warning as you like. You're nothing but a small irritation that can be easily eradicated. And don't you forget it.'' He rose to his feet and strode away from the table with his dark head elevated and his back as stiff as a ramrod.

Andrew wondered if Curtis's uncompromising rage could be the basis of the threatening terror that Trish held deep in her unconsciousness. Was he responsible in some way for what had happened to her?

Trish and Janelle were just leaving the powder room when they met Darlene. ''I wondered where you two were. We're getting ready to acknowledge Patricia's safe return with a toast and a special dance before we cut the cake.''

''No.'' Trish shook her head. ''I can't take that kind of spotlight.''

''Of course you can. Everyone wants to wish you well.'' Her tone was so false it turned Trish's stomach.

''I've lost my memory, Darlene, not my mind,'' Trish said coldly. ''Your guests are here to be entertained by my presence. You know it and I know it. You gave the party in the hopes of catching me off guard, and I agreed to come because I hoped that something or someone would trigger my lost memory. Unfortunately, we're both doomed to disappointment it seems.''

''You can't leave now,'' Darlene flared, angrily.

"Watch me." Trish brushed past Darlene before she could protest.

"I guess you told her," Janelle said as they headed back to the table. "Well, anyway, the evening isn't a bust. I saw you and Andrew dancing. Wow, the sizzle sparking off you two could start a fire. You must really like the guy. Is this serious?"

"How can I be serious about anyone?" she answered honestly. "Especially someone I don't want to hurt."

"Well, Curtis seems willing to pick up where you guys left off." She eyed Trish. "Maybe you shouldn't burn all your bridges with him."

"They're already burnt," Trish said flatly, and was relieved to see Andrew sitting alone at the table.

"I guess I'd better go find Curtis. He's probably at the bar," said Janelle with a sigh. "Why is it some women have fellows to throw away and the rest of us have to be content with the leavings?" There was bitter edge to her voice that Trish had never heard before.

When Andrew rose to hold Trish's chair, she shook her head. "Let's go."

"Good idea." He kept a guiding hand on her arm as they began to weave their way out of the crowded room. They were unable to avoid the many guests who tried to stop her for a chat.

"Patricia, how lovely to see you."

"We must get together soon."

"It's a terrible time for you, we know."

None of the smiling, concerned, or curious faces brought even a flicker of recognition. Trish's smile was stiff and forced until they finally made their way to the front entrance.

They hurried outside and were waiting for their limousine when two men in business suits approached them.

Trish instantly recognized one of them. Lieutenant O'Donnel looked out of place in his wrinkled trousers and sports jacket, and the expression on his face was not one of joviality.

When the detective saw Trish, he said something quickly to a younger and taller man who hurried inside the building while O'Donnel came over to Trish and Andrew.

He gave them both a reserved nod. "I understand that there's a celebration going on, honoring your safe return, Ms. Radcliffe."

She nodded, puzzled. "Were you invited, Lieutenant?"

"Oh, no, this is official business. We came to talk with Mrs. Perry Reynolds. We have some news about her husband."

Trish swallowed hard. His expression didn't indicate anything positive. Her voice was thin and shaky as she asked, "What kind of news?"

He kept his sharp eyes fixed on her face. "It seems that the coast guard found a small cruiser floating aimlessly on the current, several hundred miles out to sea. They towed it back to shore and made a startling discovery."

As if some awareness deep in her subconscious knew what he was going to say, Trish leaned against Andrew for support.

"The body of Perry Reynolds was found floating in the water-logged cabin. Only he didn't drown. He was killed by a bullet through the head."

Chapter Thirteen

Trish stared at Lieutenant O'Donnel like someone suddenly gone deaf and dumb. Her mind denied the relevancy of his words, and something deep and powerful within her refused to relate to their meaning. A protective mental barrier fell into place, separating her from the destructive shock.

Andrew was the one who reacted. "You mean he committed suicide?"

"That seems unlikely, since we didn't find a gun in the cabin." His steady eyes never left Trish's face. "We did find some other things, though. Why don't we go down to the station and have a little chat, Ms. Radcliffe? I'm sure you'll want to hear all the particulars."

She fought to suppress a shiver. *Why was he looking at her like that?* The reality of the situation suddenly hit her like an Arctic chill. *Perry Reynolds was dead and the detective believed she already knew it.* With a choked sob, Trish pressed her hands tightly against the side of her head.

Andrew tightened his arm around her waist and glared at O'Donnel. "She needs time to absorb the shock. Maybe tomorrow—"

He shook his head. "No. In a situation like this, time is not a luxury. She'll have to answer some questions for us tonight."

"She doesn't have any answers," Andrew flared. "Can't you guys get it through your thick skulls that she can't remember. That's what amnesia is," he added sarcastically.

O'Donnel didn't even blink at the implied insult. He just nodded. "Maybe something will jog Ms. Radcliffe's memory. In any case, we'll have to try and find some answers."

Andrew knew from his tone that there wasn't any use arguing. He glanced at Trish's glazed expression and cursed the insensitivity of the law. Their limousine was already waiting at the curb, so Andrew said, "All right," and propelled Trish toward the limo. "What station?"

"Why don't I ride along with you and leave my car for my partner who will be bringing Mrs. Reynolds along?"

The suggestion was more an order than a request, and the lieutenant's polite tone didn't fool Andrew one bit. If they turned down O'Donnel's suggestion, he might have ordered Trish in the police cruiser and ended the argument right then and there.

The three of them sat in silence for most of the trip back to Manhattan. If O'Donnel was impressed by the luxurious limousine, he didn't show it. Most of the time, he sat with his hands folded on his generous middle, and let his gaze shift from Trish's stunned expression to Andrew's glaring frown.

As they neared the police station, warmth began to flow back into Trish's chilled body, and a blessed detachment from the horror of the moment was replaced by a sense of panic.

"It's going to be all right," Andrew soothed as the hand he held suddenly began to tremble.

She scarcely heard him. Her ears were filled with an inner tumult. *You have to remember. You have to remember.*

At the station, O'Donnel quickly escorted them into a small interrogation room. Trish paid little attention to the surroundings. She heard Andrew protesting the manner of the interrogation, but O'Donnel referred to the situation as "a little chat."

"You can stay with her as long as you keep your mouth shut," O'Donnel told Andrew in a tone that brooked no argument.

Trish sat down in a wooden chair beside Andrew and struggled to maintain an inner equilibrium that was tilting like an off-balance gyroscope.

O'Donnel began asking her the same kinds of questions that he'd asked before, and she gave the same answers.

"When was the last time you saw Perry Reynolds?"

"I don't remember."

"Was he with you the day of the storm?"

"I don't remember."

"Did you kill him?" The question came at her with the swiftness of a dagger.

Her breath caught. The floor seemed to waver beneath her chair as she whispered the same answer in choked horror, "I don't remember."

"That's it!" Andrew was on his feet. "You can do your badgering when she has legal counsel, and not before. We're out of here." He tried to urge Trish to her feet, but she just sat there, her eyes fixed on O'Donnel.

"Why did you ask me that?"

The detective hesitated. "Maybe your friend is right. We should save this until you have legal representation, Ms. Radcliffe."

"Please, I have to know. Tell me everything. What makes you think I could have...been responsible?"

Andrew wanted to protest but her insistence was so compelling that he could only sit back down and capture her hand again in his. He knew that she was fighting to recover any tiny piece of herself, even if the truth threatened to destroy her. Being devoid of any past memories was already a dire sentence to endure.

O'Donnel folded his hands on the table. "We found a woman's purse in the cabin."

Her lips were stiff. "Mine?"

He nodded.

"Are you sure? I mean, women's purses are all alike. It could belong to someone else," she protested.

"This one contains your wallet and identification. Would you like to see it?"

She shook her head. Why bother? It wouldn't be any more familiar than any of the other things that supposedly belonged to her.

"Do you own a gun, Ms. Radcliffe?"

She sighed. "I don't know."

"We'll check for a registration, of course."

Andrew's stomach took a sickening plunge. If Trish did own a registered gun and the bullet that killed Perry was of the same caliber, Lieutenant O'Donnel would have the evidence he needed. Andrew didn't believe for one moment that Trish would kill anyone, but the circumstantial evidence mounting against her was frightening.

"Trish, let's get out of here." Every moment they stayed could stiffen any charges they might want to make against her.

"Maybe you should seek legal counsel before we talk again," O'Donnel conceded, making no objection to Andrew's rush to get Trish out of the room. "Stay close where we can reach you."

Andrew propelled her down the hall, and had just reached the front desk when Darlene came in, escorted by the other policemen who had been with O'Donnel earlier.

When Darlene saw Trish, she screamed and jabbed her finger at her. "Why did you kill him? Wasn't the money enough for you? He was going to end the whole thing. That was it, wasn't it? You'd rather kill him than give him up."

Andrew maneuvered Trish past the nearly hysterical woman. Her vile accusations followed them out the door, filling the night air with her fury.

Only Andrew's support kept Trish moving down the steps to the waiting limousine. Before the driver could get out of the front seat and make it around the car, Andrew had the door open and was urging Trish inside. The chauffeur shot an anxious glance at Trish as she huddled in the back seat.

"Where to, sir?" he asked Andrew as he prepared to shut the door after them.

Andrew hesitated. He wasn't sure if he should take Trish home or find some place where she could collect herself. He could tell that Trish was only holding on to her emotions by a force of will. Darlene's verbal attack had added another dimension to O'Donnel's accusing interrogation.

"Let's take a turn through the park while we decide," Andrew told the driver.

"No," Trish objected forcibly. A trapped feeling sent panic racing through her. Suddenly the interior of the car was too confining. None of her nightmares had been as terrifying as the fears that were swelling up inside of her. She wanted to run and hide from everything and everyone. Undefined images whirled in her head, and she heard O'Donnel's voice ricocheting from one side of her skull to the other, beating her with questions she couldn't answer. She reached for the door handle. "Let me out!"

Andrew pulled her back and barked at the driver. "Home."

Home...home...home. The word was like a foreign sound to her, having no meaning and no context. She had been told where she lived, where she belonged, but none of the beliefs were hers. She had accepted what everyone told her as the truth. Now two people were telling her that she had murdered someone. How could she defend herself when she wasn't even sure that what they were saying was not the truth?

Andrew circled his arms around her in a protective embrace. He could sense the wild beating of her heart as fear sent adrenaline racing through her. Without saying anything he tried to honor her feelings. This was not the time for spouting empty platitudes that everything was all right. Hell, things couldn't be worse, he silently swore. He was ready to go to battle with someone, but who? The only thing he was sure about was that Trish had every right to be afraid for her own life.

Letting her head rest against Andrew's chest, Trish closed her eyes and swallowed back choked whimpers. The regular rhythm of his breathing was strangely reassuring and by the time the limousine pulled up in front of her building, her panic had slightly subsided.

Andrew's admiration for her deepened when he saw her assume an air of composure as she nodded at the doorman and they entered the foyer. As they walked toward the elevators, he debated with himself whether he should insist on staying with her until Janelle got home. He was startled when Trish stopped short in the middle of the foyer, almost as if she'd run into an invisible wall.

''What is it? What's the matter?''

Without answering, she turned and walked right back outside. He was at her side in a second. ''What is it?''

She looked at him, clear-eyed and steady. ''I want to go home with you.''

After the emotional shock she had endured, he hadn't been sure what to expect. He smiled in relief. ''Sounds like a good idea. Do you want to pack a bag first?''

''No.''

He didn't argue, but slipped his arm through hers as they walked to where he had parked his car. They could have been two people out for an early stroll, all dressed up for a dinner party. He glanced at her calm profile, and in some ways there was something about her stiff, controlled manner that was more disturbing than the panic she'd displayed in the limo. Was she retreating into some protective state where he might not be able to reach her? Maybe it would be a good idea to call Dr. Duboise in the morning. After what had just happened, the doctor might want him to bring her to Havengate for a special session.

Trish sat close beside him as they drove to the cottage. He turned the radio to soft music, the kind they had danced to just a few hours earlier. Remembering the sensuous way they had moved together, and the inviting curves of her body nestled against his, he knew that having her stay the night with him was going to present some challenges. He had cared tenderly for her when she first came into his life, and his feelings for her had deepened and expanded. No telling how rough the road was that lay ahead, but any sacrifice would be worth it if he could keep her happily in his life.

As they climbed the stairs to the deck, she said in a strained voice, ''I think I'll just stay out here a bit.''

''All right.'' He couldn't even imagine what was going through her mind, but he accepted her need to be alone. ''I'll put on some coffee.''

She could hear him moving around the house as she leaned against the railing and looked out at the rippling sheen of moonlight on the water. A rhythmic surf, ebbing and flowing against the beach below, lent a soothing touch to her jangled nerves. Somewhere a night bird made a soft piping cheep as if calling to a mate.

The soft night sounds allowed Trish to withdraw to some protective corner of her mind where she could handle the devastating news that O'Donnel had laid on her. Perry Reynolds was dead. He'd died from a bullet to his head. Her purse had been found in the cabin with his body, and Lieutenant O'Donnel believed that she'd killed her business partner.

This wasn't happening, she told herself, struggling

to deny the harsh reality enveloping her. She wanted to flee and hide herself away, but where could she go? There was no escape from the shackles of her lost memory.

The only image that had broken through the blank curtain of her memory was the fleeting image of a gray-haired man whom they said was her business partner. Why? Why was he the one person she remembered. Was it because she already knew that Perry Reynolds was dead?

Andrew had just finished making some fresh coffee when the phone rang. He picked up the receiver, and, for some reason, wasn't surprised to hear Curtis's angry voice.

"Is Patricia there with you?"

"Yes." Andrew waited for the expected explosive response.

"I want to speak with her."

"I'm sorry, she's taking a little quiet time for herself right now."

"Do I have to drive all the way to your place tonight to see her?" he demanded in a haughty tone.

"I wouldn't advise it. It's quite late to make that trip for nothing," Andrew said evenly. "Trish has made it clear that at the moment she doesn't want to see any of you."

"Don't you realize that you're jeopardizing a very perilous situation?" he snapped. "There are important decisions that have to be made. I should think that you'd be eager to help protect Patricia in this situation."

"I am. And that's why you'll have to wait until tomorrow to disturb her. Good night." He hung up the phone with a punctuating bang.

When Andrew went out on the deck, Trish resisted the temptation to forget about everything but being here with him. She turned around as he joined her at the railing, and in a soft voice pleaded, "You're the only one I can trust, Andrew. Tell me what to believe."

He was taken back for a moment. How much of the confusion in his own mind should he share?

"Please, be honest with me."

He took a deep breath. "All right, I can do that. First of all, you have to believe in yourself. Trust your gut feelings. Don't let anyone dictate to you what you believe or don't believe."

"How can I do that when I have to depend on other people to tell me who I am?"

"That's not true. Deep down, you know who you are. That's what you need to trust."

"I'm not sure I can."

"Of course, you can. Despite the fact that your memory has failed you, you can't be anybody else but you. You're this lovely woman standing beside me right this moment. Complete. Whole."

Her lips trembled as she looked out upon the ocean that stretched into the dark rim of the horizon. "The only time I feel whole and complete is when I'm with you."

"That's because I know without a doubt that you are the true victim in this situation."

She shivered as she pictured a small white boat rocking aimlessly with the current. "What do you think happened? Why did I end up here on this beach when I must have been with Perry on the boat during the storm?"

"We don't know, for sure, that you were there," he

said quickly, even though he had failed to come up with any other scenario in his own mind. She'd been terrified when he found her on the beach, and her hysterical amnesia must have had its basis in what had happened during the storm. If she had been on the boat with Perry, she might have made it to shore in the condition he found her.

As if reading his mind, she said in a leaden tone. "Nothing else makes sense, does it? Do you think I killed him?"

"Do you think you did?"

"Don't play Dr. Duboise with me," she flared. "Always asking a question instead of answering mine."

"All right," he chuckled, surprised and pleased at her sudden display of spunk. "No, I don't think you shot Perry Reynolds. I doubt that you even know how to handle a gun. If I handed you one right now, you probably wouldn't even know how to release the safety catch."

A spurt of hope shot through her, and then just as quickly died. "Maybe I did know how to use a gun once, but I've forgotten just like everything else."

"That's not likely. Remember, Dr. Duboise explained that you could lose personal memories in hysterical amnesia without any functional knowledge being lost? You remembered how to drive a car, use a computer and a dozen other things like that. If you knew how to handle a gun once, you still would."

"O'Donnel would never believe I was telling the truth."

"Probably not, but *you* would know whether or not handling a gun is familiar. And that's what's important. You have to honor your feelings. Deep down you know what is true, and you're going to have to hold on to that, Trish.'' His voice softened as he added, ''There's one more thing.''

''What is that?''

''I don't want you to trust anybody, except me.''

''I don't think that will be too difficult. Of course, I would like a little proof of your sincerity.''

''Like what?''

''You'll think of something.'' Impulsively, she leaned into him as her hands slipped up around his neck.

The way she was searching his face, he knew that if he rejected the love she offered, all the words about his being there for her would count for nothing. Even though one kiss could open a flood of desire that neither of them would be able to close, he couldn't turn away. She wanted him, and he wanted her, and at the moment all his reasons for holding back faded. Whatever the future or the past held, he was committed to loving her, and she needed to know that.

He brushed a kiss to her forehead, and then lowered his lips to find hers. Trish trembled in his arms, matching the rising hunger of his desire as his hands slipped from her waist to draw her closer. There was no need for words as they delighted in the rising passion that crowded out every thought but the promised pleasure that awaited them.

''Shall we go inside?'' she asked breathlessly.

''The coffee will get cold.''

She gave a soft laugh as he led her inside to the bedroom that had been her refuge and comfort.

As they lay together, all ugliness in the world faded away, and she marveled at the suspended bliss his kisses and touch created in her. His tender caresses and softly spoken endearments healed her spirit, and the incredible sensations of making love gave her back a confidence that she had nearly lost.

As Andrew traced the lines and curves of her sweet naked loveliness, he was filled with the wonder of having found a woman who was totally without pretense. Every response she made to his touch was honest and in harmony with his needs. The explosive fulfillment of their desire was one that neither of them had experienced before.

Content and satiated with love, they lay quietly in each other's arms, and neither the past nor the future had any reality or any relevancy. They were lovers who had found each other, and for the moment they jealously clung to the reprieve that had been given them.

Chapter Fourteen

Andrew awoke early, even before the first blush of gray light touched the ocean with the shiny patina of a new day. Trish was curled up beside him, and for a long moment, he lay still, savoring the warmth of her soft body. She was breathing quietly in a relaxed sleep. He wanted to kiss her and let his fingers trail through her soft hair, but he resisted. The night they'd spent together had held a promise for both of them, but he knew that once she awakened, all of the torment would come rushing back. Better let her sleep, he schooled himself.

But as he slipped quietly out of bed, she stirred, opened a sleepy eye and mumbled, "Is it morning?"

"No." He leaned over and kissed her forehead. "Go ahead and sleep, love."

She sighed, closed her eyes, and her lips parted in a contented softness. He was tempted to crawl back in bed with her, but he knew he wouldn't be satisfied just to hold her in his arms while she slept.

Since it was too early for his morning walk on the beach, he decided to make a trip to an all-night market. A quick check of the fridge had been disheartening. What kind of a breakfast could they make out of one stale bagel? He didn't know what lay ahead for the rest of the day, but he knew they needed a good breakfast to handle it.

As he drove, he tried to order his thoughts. It was a sure bet that the police weren't going to leave Patricia Radcliffe alone. The inquiry into Perry's death had just begun, and she was already at the center of their attention. If she didn't cooperate they would treat her as a hostile suspect.

The first thing he needed to do was telephone Dr. Duboise. Andrew was certain that when he told the doctor about the latest developments, he would want to see Trish as soon as possible, hopefully later in the morning. As for his own work, somehow he'd have to put everything on hold and hope that his boss would be cooperative.

TRISH AWOKE SUDDENLY with a pungent odor filling her nostrils. She pushed herself up from the pillow, and struggled out of the bed, wearing only one of Andrew's T-shirts. As her nose filled up with an acrid odor, she gasped for air.

Gas!

The whole bedroom was filled with it. She could hear the hiss of escaping gas from the kitchen. *I have to get out, now!* In a few minutes the whole house would be filled. Her legs would barely hold her as she lurched across the floor to the front room. Already her head felt as if it were floating away. An enveloping wave of feebleness sent her down to her knees, and she knew that in another moment she would be lying flat on the floor, unable to get up.

She edged across the floor on her hands and knees until she reached a fireplace stand that held a brass poker, and with a last miraculous surge of strength, she took the poker, rose up on her knees and broke the nearest window flanking the fireplace. She closed her eyes against shattered glass flying in the air and crumbled to the floor as unconsciousness like a black rolling wave overtook her.

ANDREW SAW THE BROKEN window as soon as he bounded up the deck steps. "What in the—?" Then he smelled the odor of gas escaping from the house.

"Trish! Trish!" he shouted as he opened the front door. He coughed from the onslaught of gas, and his eyes smarted from the biting fumes.

Stepping inside, he saw with horror Trish's unconscious body lying in a pool of broken glass. Coughing and gagging, he carried her out of house and laid her down a safe distance away. She was unconscious but still breathing. Jerking his cell phone out of its carrier on his belt, he dialed 911.

He knew he was shouting at the operator but he couldn't stop himself. "Send an ambulance. My house is filled with gas and I have someone who's unconscious." He gave directions to his bungalow and pleaded, "Hurry, hurry."

He stayed on the line and answered the woman's questions as rationally as his total terror would allow. It seemed like an excruciating eternity before the paramedics arrived. He tried to stay out of the way as an efficient team examined Trish and quickly loaded her on a gurney. The driver motioned for Andrew to get into the ambulance with Trish, and quickly slammed the door as the two paramedics worked over her.

The emergency office must have alerted the gas company because Andrew glimpsed the utilities truck arriving just as the ambulance was leaving. They took Trish to the nearest hospital, a small facility about ten minutes away, and even before they arrived at the emergency entrance, she was responding to the oxygen mask placed over her nose and mouth.

As she opened her eyes, her bewildered gaze swept around the ambulance. Andrew was close enough to touch her, and with as much reassurance in his voice as his tumbling insides would allow, he said, "I'm here, darling. It's okay. You're going to be fine."

At the hospital they whisked Trish into the emergency room, leaving Andrew standing helplessly in the middle of the reception area until an intake nurse motioned him over to the admittance desk.

"We'll need some information," she said, a tired smile reflected in her eyes. She handed him a clipboard with some papers clipped to it. "Fill out as much as you can."

The first form was just routine information, which Andrew handled as best he could. He stared at the second sheet, asking him to fill out a report about what had happened to cause the patient to require emergency treatment.

He stared at the form. He was clueless about what had happened. Trish had been asleep when he left. Had a gas line broken and the smell alerted her? There was no gas smell in the house before he'd left for the store.

He ran an agitated hand through his hair. The sun still hadn't come up by the time he got back to the house, so he couldn't have been gone very long. He couldn't add up what had happened to make any kind of sense. He left the second form blank and handed the clipboard back to the nurse.

"When can I see her?" Andrew demanded in an impatient tone.

"Why don't you have a seat. As soon as I have some information, I'll let you know."

He could tell from the nurse's set jaw that there was no use in arguing.

Andrew sat slumped in an uncomfortable chair for nearly an hour before a young intern suddenly appeared before him. Instantly Andrew stiffened as his eyes searched the young man's face for some clue as to what he was going to say.

"Ms. Radcliffe has been taken to a private room, and you can see her now."

"How is she?"

"She's one lucky lady. We expect her to make a full recovery within twenty-four hours. Until then, we'll keep her here for observation." He smiled at Andrew. "Take it easy. At the moment, you look worse than she does."

Trish must have thought the same thing, because she sent Andrew a reassuring smile through the plastic walls of an oxygen tent. She was obviously drained and weak, and her arms lay limply at her sides. His heart lurched in his chest as she mouthed the words, "I love you."

His eyes grew moist with relief, and he gave her a loving smile that needed no words of explanation. She smiled back, and closed her eyes, too weary to keep them open another moment.

He sat beside her bed for nearly an hour until the nurse reassured him that Trish would probably sleep most of the day, and suggested that he come back later when the patient was ready for some company.

"Unless there are complications, she'll be dismissed tomorrow," the nurse had reassured him.

Unless there are complications. The words kept rolling over and over in his mind like a hamster wheel as he drove back to the cottage. He was oblivious to the sunny new day that had held such promise only a few hours ago. The wonderful breakfast he'd been planning on making was a mockery in the crisis that had engulfed them. His stomach was so taut, he wondered if he'd ever want to eat again.

When he pulled off the road into his short driveway, he was surprised to see a New Jersey police car parked beside the utility truck. Was this a routine call? Maybe his cottage wasn't the only one having gas problems.

All the windows and doors in the house had been opened, but the acidic smell of gas lingered strongly as he got out of his car. Two service men came around the back of the house, and when they saw Andrew, they came over to him.

"There's a policeman around back. He wants to talk with you," said an older man, peering through his glasses.

"Did you get the gas leak fixed?" Andrew asked anxiously.

The two men exchanged glances, and the gray-haired man shoved his glasses back on his nose with an impatient gesture. "There wasn't any leak."

"Then what happened?"

"The stove valves were turned on full force. The pilot light was out."

"What?" A sickening churning began in the pit of Andrew's stomach.

"You'd better be talking to the policeman. We're done here." As they walked away, Andrew heard him say to his young assistant. "Don't be talking about this, understand? The policeman said that this whole thing will probably end up in court and we'll have to testify."

Andrew knew the truth then. The gas-filled house had been no accident. The paranoia that Trish had been fighting since the first moment he'd found her had been validated by this deliberate intent to kill her.

He stood there several minutes, looking at the bungalow as his mind raced to handle the unspeakable truth. Whoever it was must have been watching the house for a long time. They knew that she was there, and when he drove away, carelessly leaving the house unlocked for the few minutes he was gone. The way was clear for someone to slip in and turn on the gas stove burners.

Andrew walked with weighted steps around to the back of the house, and came face-to-face with a lean, tall policeman who was just coming down the stairs.

"Mr. Davis? I'm Officer Baxley." He smiled as if this was a normal meeting and not something out of a bizarre crime novel.

"Yes, Officer, I'm the house's owner. I just got back from the hospital."

"And how is the lady in question?" he asked politely.

"Good. They expect her to be released tomorrow."

"Well, that's promising news. Sometime these things have a way of working out for the best. Of course, in a case like this, there has to be some follow-up, you know."

"I would hope so," Andrew said shortly. "When someone deliberately plots murder, and almost succeeds, I would expect more than a follow-up."

''Murder?'' Officer Baxley looked puzzled.

''What else do you call it? Someone entered the house while I was gone, turned on the gas and left, expecting my houseguest to be killed in her sleep.''

The policeman shook his head. ''I'm afraid that you have the wrong idea of what happened here, Mr. Davis. It wasn't attempted murder.'' He held up the plastic-covered piece of paper. ''This note makes it clear. This was attempted suicide.''

After a moment of absolute stunned silence, Andrew felt hysterical laughter building in his chest. ''You can't be serious.''

''Dead serious. We found this on a kitchen counter.''

''Let me see it.''

The officer hesitated and then nodded. ''You can read it through the plastic, but don't take it out.''

Andrew stared at the short typed note in utter disbelief.

I'm sorry. I can't go on pretending. I didn't mean to kill Perry.

''No, there's some mistake.'' Andrew thrust the note back at him.

''I know this is a shock to you,'' Baxley said in a knowing manner, as if lovers' quarrels were a part of his unhappy job.

''Yes, a shock,'' Andrew agreed with tight lips.

''The lady must have changed her mind at that last minute, and tried to get out of the house.''

There were too many inconsistencies, but it was no use arguing with this policeman who had no idea of the drama that preceded this pseudo-suicide scam. Andrew knew he needed time to line up the facts and present them to Lieutenant O'Donnel.

TRISH WAS OUT OF THE oxygen tent later that afternoon when Janelle rushed into the room, bringing an overnight bag.

"Andrew called me at the office." Janelle's worried eyes searched Trish's pale face. "He said there'd been a gas leak at the cottage. How awful! Are you all right? Everyone's worried to death. How did something like that happen?"

"I don't know," Trish said honestly. "I just woke up and the house was filled with gas. I guess a gas line broke in the kitchen."

"And where was Andrew?" she asked in a critical tone. "Curtis told me Andrew took you to his place for the night. Really, Trish. Why are you so blasted trusting?"

"It wasn't Andrew's fault," Trish said defensively. "He'd gone to the store to get some things for breakfast. Anyway, he came back in time."

"Thank heavens for that! Darlene was furious that her party was ruined. She put the blame on you. She's been telling everyone that you were seeing a psychiatrist and your behavior had been terribly erratic since your return." Janelle sighed. "Curtis wasn't too happy about the whole thing, either."

"I'm sorry. I just couldn't stand being on display like that."

Janelle reached over and patted her hand. "It's all right, honey. I told Darlene the party was a bad idea in the first place, but she had some crazy idea that—" Janelle hesitated.

"I know. Darlene wanted to catch me remembering someone or something," Trish finished.

Janelle nodded. "Makes you wonder just how much stuff she and Gary are covering up themselves."

Trish didn't answer. Suddenly she was too tired to even listen to any more speculation. Thankfully, a moment later she heard Andrew's voice in the hall, and her fatigue instantly lessened. Drawing on the memory of the night they'd spent together, a warm flush eased through her as he came through the door. He was smiling and carrying a bouquet of pink roses.

Ignoring Janelle, he leaned over the bed and kissed Trish gently. "How you doing, love?"

"Better." Her eyes added a message of their own as she smiled lovingly at him.

As if embarrassed to be a third party in the charged energy between them, Janelle reached for the flowers. "Here let me put them in water." She left the room to ask a nurse for a vase.

Andrew down sat on the edge of the bed. "Your blood tests are normal. You're one lucky lady," he said thankfully.

"What happened? Did they find the gas leak?"

Somehow he had to delay telling her that what had happened was no accident. He had talked to Dr. Dubois and the doctor agreed that it would be best for Trish to be at Havengate when she learned that someone had tried to kill her and frame her for Perry's murder with a suicide note.

"Yes, they found the leak, but the house still smells of gas. What do think about spending a couple of nights at Havengate while it airs out?"

His casual suggestion didn't ring true. Her eyes narrowed. "You've talked to Duboise about this, haven't you? What aren't you telling me?"

Instead of answering her last question, he parried, "Dr. Duboise and I agree that after this kind of experience, you need some down time. Your old room is ready and waiting. Wouldn't you rather spend the night there than here?"

She searched his face and saw only a loving concern in his eyes. He was worried, that was obvious. This whole miserable happening had obviously taken a toll on him. She felt guilty for being the object of another emotional drain on him.

"All right," she said wearily. "Whatever you say."

When Janelle came back with the flowers, they told her what had been arranged. "Oh, I was thinking that I could vacate the guest bedroom, and you and Andrew could stay at the apartment," she said. "What do you think?"

Trish looked at Andrew hopefully, but he shook his head. "Maybe in a day or two. We'll see."

The way he said it, Trish had the feeling that her stay at Havengate wasn't going to be the overnight visit that he had proposed. This suspicion increased as they made the transfer in his car from the small hospital to Havengate.

"So nice to see you again," beamed Ms. Sloan as if Trish were an old friend returning for a visit. "Dr. Duboise left word that he'd be willing to see you tonight if necessary."

Necessary? Trish looked at Andrew, and knew from his closed expression that there was something he wasn't telling her. *What was going on? Were they somehow blaming her for what had happened?*

As Trish and Andrew walked across the grounds

from the admittance building to her room, she felt like someone trying to discern the shape and size of a threatening force waiting to leap out at her.

She shivered. "Something's terribly wrong, isn't it? Have they found more proof that I was with Perry on the boat? That I shot him?"

"No," he said forcibly. "Quit thinking like that."

He was furious that she was being set up by someone. The false suicide note was evidence of that.

"You're holding something back," she accused him, fighting a familiar stab of uneasiness settling bone-deep within her.

If Andrew had been sure of her emotional reaction, he would have told her right then and there that someone had followed them to his cottage and waited for the opportunity to kill her—or maybe both of them. But he couldn't ignore the way she was looking at him like a frightened animal crowded into a corner. She'd be better off in Dr. Duboise's hands when she learned the truth.

He pulled her into his arms and they clung to each other for a long moment. He stroked her hair and whispered, "We'll find the answer to all of this. I promise."

He refrained from telling her the one thing that was certain.

That the discovery of Perry's body had sent a killer into action.

Chapter Fifteen

When Andrew kissed Trish goodbye, he could tell that she was bewildered to find herself back at Havengate. Even though she didn't know the truth about her narrow escape, she was understandably shaken up by the experience.

"Call me if you can't sleep," he said gently. "And we'll stay awake together."

"Only if you promise I can come back to the cottage after I see Dr. Duboise tomorrow," she bargained.

"The cottage isn't smelling all that sweet at the moment. Maybe we should think about me being your houseguest for a while," he suggested casually. Until some protection had been arranged for her, he wasn't going to let her out of his sight.

Her eyes smiled at him. "I've got a queen-size bed."

"Well, I guess we can always use half of it." He grinned.

ANDREW RETURNED TO THE cottage just after dusk and was startled to see all the lights on, and three cars parked at the side of the house. He recognized the police car that Officer Baxley had been driving that morning, but the other two unmarked cars had New York license plates.

Good, thought Andrew. When he had called Lieutenant O'Donnel earlier in the day, the policeman had listened to everything Andrew had to say without showing much excitement or interest.

"Don't you see what this means?" Andrew had demanded impatiently. "Someone is trying to set Trish up for Perry's murder."

"Take it easy, son. No need to be jumping to a lot of hasty conclusions without looking at things from more than one side. Where'd you say your place was?"

"On the beach just a few miles across the New Jersey state line." He told him the quickest way to get there.

"That's out of my jurisdiction," O'Donnel replied curtly. "Of course, if Patricia Radcliffe's attempted suicide has something to do with my ongoing case, we'll work something out with the New Jersey authorities."

"She didn't attempt suicide," Andrew flared. "That's what I'm telling you. Any idiot can see that!"

O'Donnel had made some noncommittal comments and hung up. Andrew didn't know whether or not the detective was going to do his own investigation or just rely on Baxley's report.

As he bounded toward the front steps of the cottage, he saw that a yellow banner designating a crime scene had been stretched across the front, and a redheaded man was kneeling at the front door with a fingerprint kit.

Hallelujah, thought Andrew. O'Donnel was taking

the matter seriously. He ducked under the paper barrier, and the crime lab officer let him get by when Andrew assured him that he lived there.

Both O'Donnel and Baxley were in the kitchen. The two officers were a sharp contrast in appearance. Baxley's youthful tall, beanpole frame barely filled out his roomy uniform, while O'Donnel's hefty middle-aged stoutness tugged at his brown tweed suit. From the way the two men looked at him as he came in, Andrew sensed that they had formed a united front in the investigation. Andrew felt a soft brush of fear creeping up his spine. Surely they agreed that the suicide setup was a deadly hoax, didn't they?

"I'm glad you're both here," he said as he gave them a nod of greeting. "It's a relief to know you're taking this thing seriously, Lieutenant."

"Oh, I'm taking it seriously," he assured Andrew. "I've checked out Officer Baxley's report. It seems pretty comprehensive. We'll wait to see if we get anything unexpected on the fingerprints."

Unexpected? The word spoke volumes. They didn't believe that anyone else had been in the house. They weren't expecting anyone's but Trish's.

"There's not much more that we can do," Baxley said as if they'd taken care of everything.

"That's it?" Andrew said in a calm voice that belied the surge of raw anger building inside. It was all he could do to keep from lashing out at them for even considering that the suicide note was valid. Trish had been set up. Couldn't these two policemen see that the whole deadly incident was contrived?

"At the moment, yes," O'Donnel answered without looking directly at Andrew.

"If the killer didn't leave fingerprints, what then?"

O'Donnel ignored his question. "After our telephone conversation, I made a few calls this morning. It seems that Ms. Radcliffe left the party in her honor rather abruptly last night. She was about to head home when I got there, wasn't she? Do you know what that was all about? Was there some kind of precipitating incident that I should know about? A quarrel with someone?"

"No, she left because she couldn't take the pressure of people gawking at her, asking her a hundred times if she remembered them."

"Then she was in a despondent mood? Feeling kind of harassed?"

"If you mean was her mood suicidal, no."

O'Donnel paused, as if trying to decide whether or not to elicit more details about the night that she had spent with Andrew. "Did you have a lovers' quarrel, perhaps?"

"No, quite the opposite."

Baxley smirked in a knowing way, but O'Donnel looked as if he had already decided that nothing Andrew said could be taken at face value.

"We'll look at this whole thing in light of what we already know about Ms. Radcliffe," he said flatly, putting an end to the discussion.

The lieutenant didn't have to spell it out for Andrew. He knew exactly what he meant. O'Donnel was talking about the Perry Reynold's murder. The suicide note could be one more piece of evidence in the case. Trish's purse on the boat had already provided opportunity in Perry Reynold's murder. Now she was a suspect whose emotional and mental health was in question. The suicide attempt and note, however bogus, supported his case. Why look for a different killer when someone was handing Trish to him on a silver platter?

O'Donnel must have seen the fury rising in Andrew because he quickly assured him, "We're looking into all aspects of Perry Reynolds's death. We've got a court order to examine all the books at Atlantis Enterprises. Maybe something will come to light that will clarify this whole situation."

Andrew didn't trust himself to answer. He knew what O'Donnel was looking for—evidence that would give him the motive he needed to charge Trish with first-degree murder.

FROM THE MOMENT THAT Trish entered Dr. Duboise's office, she knew that this wasn't going to be one of their usual sessions. Normally he eased into their time together with some friendly banter, and asked some superficial questions about her well-being. He had always seemed willing to let the session develop without any apparent structure, but that was not the case this time. He was more purposeful about leading the conversation, as if he had an intended goal in mind.

Her guard went up, and because she felt she was being manipulated toward some end that she didn't understand, she was hesitant about volunteering anything. Was he laying the groundwork for keeping her at Havengate more than just a day or two?

"You had a harrowing experience." His tone was matter-of-fact, but there was something about his body language that didn't match.

His pretended lack of concern made her voice sharp. "Andrew told you what happened, didn't he?"

He nodded. "Don't you want to tell me about it?"

"Not really," she said, with a slightly pugnacious attitude.

"You smelled gas when you first woke up? That must have been scary."

She made him pull every bit of the story out of her, piece by piece. "There was a gas leak...a pipe in the kitchen. I could hear it."

There were long pauses when she didn't say anything, and she sensed that the doctor was fighting some kind of impatience of his own. Usually his hands rested on the arm of his chair, but there was a hidden restlessness in his long slender fingers that moved slightly as he waited for her to speak.

"When I couldn't get the front door open, I knew I had to break a window." She shivered as the remembered sensation of suffocation sweeping over her.

"Because you wanted to save your life."

She stared at him in disbelief. "Of course I wanted to save my life. What kind of a question is that?" A quiver of suspicion took root that he was questioning everything that she had said.

"It's just a question," he soothed.

What was going on? Her temper flared. "You don't believe what I'm telling you."

"Yes, I believe you, Trish." His eyes firmly locked with hers. "But I'm afraid that there are some disquieting aspects about what happened that you don't know about."

She stared at him, her mouth suddenly parched. Her posture rigid and defensive as she demanded, "What is it that I know about, Dr. Duboise?"

In a very even voice, he told her that it wasn't a leaking gas pipe that had filled the house with gas.

''All of the vents on the stove had been deliberately turned on.''

The way he was looking at her made her gasp. ''But you don't think...you can't think that I...''

''You tried to kill yourself?'' he finished for her.

Even as he waited for her response, the truth came to her as clear as crystal. ''Someone tried to kill me, didn't they?''

A weird kind of validation flowed through her. She had been right all along. The insidious apprehension and fear that had tormented her had not been her imagination. Her nightmares had risen from a deep knowledge that she was in danger.

He shifted the glasses resting on his nose. ''There was a suicide note.''

''A suicide note?'' she echoed in disbelief.

He leaned forward. ''You need to be prepared to handle the stress of the police asking you some questions, Trish.''

Was this for real? Was she having another nightmare? Suddenly she was furious with Andrew. Why had he kept all of this from her? Why make her wait to hear the truth from Dr. Duboise? She'd tried to get him to share his thoughts with her, and he dodged her questions. He hadn't lied to her, but he hadn't been truthful either. Wasn't there anyone that she could trust?

The doctor said gently, ''I know this is a lot for you to take in. Is there any way we can make the situation easier for you?''

She shook her head and only half-listened to him when he suggested that they talk later, after she'd had a chance to think things through.

''Yes, thank you, Dr. Duboise.'' She walked out of

his office in a hurry to get somewhere—if she could just remember where.

ANDREW WAS WAITING FOR her in the lounge when she came out of the elevator and headed purposefully toward the front door. He had to hurry to catch up with her just outside the building.

"Trish, wait up!"

As she swung around to face him, she didn't say anything, but just looked at Andrew as if he were someone who had no business trying to pretend that everything was friendly and cozy between them.

The cold look in her eyes was a total shock to Andrew. Certainly, he had expected her to be shaken by the realization that someone had tried to kill her. In fact, he had been prepared to find her in a tearful, shattered state, in need of his comforting and reassurance. What he had not expected was her removed, distant composure. She was a stranger, and he floundered trying to decide what to do and say. As he reached to touch her arm, she drew back.

"No," she said, firmly. "Leave me alone. I can handle this."

"But, Trish, please, let me help you."

"Help me? How? By lying to me? By being a coward?"

He stiffened. "Wait a minute. Let's get something straight. I was trying to protect you by letting Dr. Duboise tell you everything. I thought he could handle things better." He softened his voice. "Darling, I know this has been a shock."

"You mean, I should be surprised that someone is trying to harm me?" She gave a false laugh. "If you want to know the truth, it's a relief to know that my paranoid feelings have been validated. I can handle a threat upon my life better than living with the horrible doubts that I was losing my sanity along with my memory. Now, you don't have to feel sorry for me anymore.''

''Stop it, Trish! You know me better than that.''

''Do I? Anyway, I can take it from here. I'm going to trust myself from now on, and I'm not going to be a sitting duck for anyone.''

''Good.'' Even though this belligerent, forceful Trish was something of a shock, Andrew couldn't help but silently applaud her declaration of independence.

''I'm checking myself out of here,'' she said in a tone that brooked no argument.

''Are you sure that's wise? I mean you're safe here.''

''Are you suggesting that I spend the rest of my life hiding out at Havengate?'' she flared.

''No, of course not, but Trish, be reasonable. Whoever is afraid that you may recover your memory will be ready to strike again.''

''And I'm supposed to cower like a frightened rabbit until O'Donnel finds enough circumstantial evidence to convict me? Thanks but no thanks. I'd rather spend my time finding some answers myself.''

''And how do you propose to do that?'' Andrew asked, entertaining a sneaking suspicion that he wasn't going to like her answer.

''I'm going back to the apartment.''

''And?''

''Janelle tried to work with me on the computer in the library, but I got confused and quit. I need to spend some time looking over the files. Maybe there's some kind of a trail that would lead me to some answers.

Whatever happened to Perry could be related to business.''

''Or to his extramarital love life,'' Andrew offered.

She nodded. ''Maybe if I start asking questions instead of struggling to answer so many of them myself, I won't have to depend on someone else finding out the truth.''

''I don't suppose you could use a volunteer computer analyst to help you dig through the files?''

She was tempted to flatly refuse his help, but if anyone could untangle the computer files, he could. ''A business arrangement?''

''Absolutely.''

She hesitated. Could she trust him to be honest with her? Would he try to keep things from her? Would she be putting herself in a vulnerable position again? And what if he found some incriminating evidence that implicated her or someone else? His determination to protect her could work against her need to hold on to her independence.

''You can set the ground rules,'' he assured her.

''Both in professional and personal areas?''

He nodded. ''The ball is in your court.''

He was giving her some space, and she was grateful for it. ''All right, I'd appreciate your help.''

''Fine. I guess you don't mind if I move into the apartment. Janelle offered the guest room, remember?'' He was relieved that she had given him an excuse to stay around her. Without letting her know the truth, he'd be her bodyguard until O'Donnel realized he needed to assign someone to protect her.

THEY CHECKED TRISH OUT of the hospital, and she had little to say on the drive into the city. When they arrived at her apartment, Sasha told them that Janelle had gone back to her own place.

Good, thought Trish. Although Janelle meant well, her hovering manner could wear on the nerves. At the moment, the last thing she needed was someone clucking over her like a mother hen.

"I haven't any idea how much time this is going to take," she told Andrew as they walked to the library. "I don't want you to get behind on your own work."

"No problem. I'm waiting on approval for the next step in my program, anyway. Let's see how it goes." He smiled at her. "We'll have to go on a fishing expedition first, since we really don't know what we're looking for."

He settled down at the desk, and in a few minutes was so completely engrossed that she could have been miles away instead of looking over his shoulder at files that made no earthly sense to her. Not wanting to burden him with questions, she decided to leave him alone, and quietly left the room.

She was about to head to the kitchen for a cup of tea when Sasha told her she had a visitor.

"Who is it?" Trish asked, her chest suddenly tight. She knew that sooner or later the police would come. The protection that Dr. Duboise had offered her at Havengate was gone. When Sasha told her it was Curtis, she gave a sigh of relief and reluctantly walked stiffly into the living room.

"Hello, Curtis," she said in a guarded voice.

He reached for her. "Honey, I just got back in town and heard. Are you all right?"

"Yes, I'm fine," she said, putting her hands on his chest and trying to push away.

He tightened his arms around her, and she stiffened

as the whiff of his hair tonic touched her nostrils. It was the same scent that had triggered the faint memory of someone with her in Central Park. Curtis. He was the one who had embraced her in front of the statue. A strange sense of relief poured through her because somewhere in the corners of her mind had been a fear that it had been Perry.

"You can't keep running away from me. We've always meant too much to each other." He tightened his embrace.

She sensed that he'd held her close like this before, but she knew with every fiber of her being that she'd never felt desire for Curtis that she felt for Andrew.

"I'm so sorry, darling. You don't deserve all of this." He seemed about ready to lower his head and kiss her.

She deliberately turned her face away. "Please, Curtis, don't—" For whatever reason she'd broken their engagement it must have been a valid one, and this knowledge gave her a strange reassurance.

"Don't what?" he said sharply. "Don't remind you that you led me to think you were ready to be Mrs. Curtis Mandel? Don't remind you that we had plans for the company?" He suddenly pushed her away, his face hard and his eyes biting into hers with an angry glint. "What kind of little game are you playing, Patricia? Is this another one of your schemes to play me for a fool?"

For a moment she felt sorry for him. Obviously, rejection wasn't something that sat easily with him. The wedding gown in her closet was evidence enough that their plans to be married had been finalized. For whatever reason she'd changed her mind, and it was obvious he had not yet forgiven her.

''Is it true what they're saying? That you tried to commit suicide?'' His tone was accusatory. ''Is this another little ploy of yours?''

She turned away without answering.

He followed her into the living room. ''It's all over the office that there was a suicide note, and Janelle said that you were alone in the house. Where was that so-called hero of yours? How do you know he hasn't set this up for some kind of extortion scheme? I've been telling you from the beginning not to trust him.''

''Curtis, please.'' His angry words were like stinging pellets.

''And why did you run away from the party like that? You were among friends. All those people came to wish you well. Dammit, somebody has to look after you.''

''You're absolutely right,'' Andrew agreed as he came through the hall doorway.

Curtis swung around like an angry bull seeing red. ''And what in the hell are you doing here? I should think you'd be ashamed to show your face after what's happened.''

''Curtis, stop it!'' Trish ordered angrily. ''Andrew is here because I asked him to help me go through my computer files so I can understand what is going on in the company.''

Curtis looked absolutely dumbfounded. ''Why would you ask a questionable stranger to do that instead of me?''

''I think the answer is obvious,'' Andrew answered for Trish. ''Someone outside the company might be in a better position to evaluate any pertinent information impersonally.''

''What kind of information?'' Curtis snapped.

"I guess we won't know until we find it."

"And what do you plan to do with this so-called pertinent information?" Curtis asked as his jaw tightened.

Trish answered, "Turn it over to the police, of course."

At that moment, the doorbell rang again, and as if entering on cue, they heard O'Donnel's voice as Sasha let him in.

Andrew moved quickly over to Trish's side. He slipped his hand in hers and could feel a cold prickling on her skin as the detective walked in.

O'Donnel's hazel eyes swept the room, and his broad face hinted at unexpected satisfaction. "Well, isn't this nice? The hospital told me you'd been released, Ms. Radcliffe, but I hadn't expected to be lucky enough to find two gentlemen keeping you company. I hope you don't mind but I've invited Mrs. Darlene Reynolds, and her stepson, Gary, to join us for a friendly little chat."

There was nothing friendly in his direct manner, and his attempt at polite amenities only made his unspoken intent more threatening.

"Well, then, why don't we all sit down and make ourselves comfortable," Trish said in a strained voice that didn't even sound like her own. She didn't know what was coming, but one thing was certain, she could feel the quagmire of suspicion thickening all around her.

Chapter Sixteen

Trish felt like a specimen mounted on a skewer as everyone sat in her living room and stared at her. Curtis's expression was glowering, Darlene's disdainful, Gary's disgusted, and O'Donnel's accusing. Only Andrew's tender look was one of support and reassurance.

"What is this all about, Lieutenant?" Curtis demanded in his usual take-charge manner. "This is a real imposition on Patricia to have everyone in her home like this." His tone indicated that everyone should clear out except himself.

"Well, now, we could have this little chat down at the station instead if everyone would rather do that," O'Donnel replied curtly.

"No," Darlene said forcefully. "Why don't you shut up, Curtis. I'm fed up with you trying to run things. Go ahead, Lieutenant, I'd like to see them all squirm."

Gary gave a short laugh. "Careful, Mama dearest, I have a feeling there's enough garbage to go around."

"You're a great one to talk. Dealing and wheeling with every bookie in town. No wonder Perry cut you off. He should have done it years ago."

"You were the one who was getting the boot—"

Curtis broke in. "Can't you two keep your mouths shut for two minutes?"

Their angry voices vibrated like a raucous cacophony in Trish's head. It was all she could do not to put her hands over her ears and shout as loudly as the rest of them. O'Donnel had settled back in his chair, willingly letting all of them go at each other.

"Can't we get on with it, Lieutenant?" Andrew broke into the verbal fray, and sent a look around the room that finally silenced everyone.

"Yes, Lieutenant," Curtis said as if he were chairman of the board, giving the officer permission to address the group. "I'm sure everyone is a little on edge, anxious to know what's on your mind."

O'Donnel shoved his glasses back on his broad nose and glanced at a small notebook in his hand. "Well, now, I have a couple of things here that might interest you folks. We found the marina where Perry Reynolds just bought his new white cruiser a day before the storm." He peered at Darlene. "I guess he didn't tell you he'd been to Anchor Marina in New Jersey to buy a boat."

"Perry never told me anything," she retorted with an indignant fling of her blond hair. "All he cared about was business and holding on to his money."

"That's for sure," Gary grumbled, for once agreeing with his stepmother.

"Speaking of money," O'Donnel said as if the thought had just occurred to him. "It seems that the people we've had looking into the books at Atlantis Enterprises have come up with some interesting inconsistencies."

Andrew stiffened. He'd only spent a few minutes

pulling up accounting sheets, but even a quick look at them had raised some questions. He saw Trish's face blanch to a chalky white as if somewhere in the dark labyrinth of her mind, the detective's words touched a memory. He reached over and took her hand, but she didn't respond to his squeeze.

"Inconsistencies?" Curtis echoed, but there was more of an edge of irritation than surprise in his voice.

"I don't see what that has to do with me," Darlene snapped. "I've never had anything to do with the business."

"Except spend the money that Dad made off of it," Gary countered. "And your endless demands for more."

"You're one to talk, Gary, you pitiful leech."

Trish leaned forward in her chair. "Would you two stop it!" Glaring at her, the two of them fell into a belligerent silence.

Trish took several quick breaths to still the racing of her heart as distorted images lying just beyond recall threatened to bubble to the surface of her mind.

O'Donnel kept his eyes on her. "Is there something you wanted to say, Ms. Radcliffe?"

She stared back at him for a long moment, and then shook her head. "No, please go on."

"Were you aware, Ms. Radcliffe, that there had been some skimming of investor funds? Close to a hundred and fifty thousand dollars in the last year alone."

She didn't know how to answer, but Curtis saved her the trouble.

"You knew, Patricia," Curtis said sharply, "I told you a month ago weeks ago that I suspected Perry was milking some of our big accounts, but you wouldn't listen.''

''That's because she was in on it!'' Darlene snapped. ''The two of them were going to take off and leave me penniless.''

O'Donnel frowned. ''And what did Ms. Radcliffe say when you told her your suspicions, Curtis?''

''She became angry and said that she didn't believe it. I insisted and she said she'd look into it.'' He glanced at Trish. ''She had just broken our engagement and I decided to let the matter drop. After all, Perry was her partner and she was the one with the most to lose if the company went under.''

The one with the most to lose. The words vibrated in Trish's head like a deadly knell.

From the ashen look on her face Andrew knew what she was thinking. Now the police had a motive for the killing, and Trish's purse on the boat had established the opportunity. All that remained was for the law to come up with a gun to prove the means.

''Have you any idea where the money might be, Lieutenant?'' Andrew asked, trying to give Trish a chance to recover from this latest blow. ''You know the old saying—follow the money to find the culprit.''

O'Donnel nodded. ''We're looking into pseudobank accounts, but, of course, the guilty one might have stashed the ill-gotten gains away in a dozen different ways.''

''But if Perry had that much money hidden somewhere, no telling who might have gone after it,'' Andrew insisted.

''I know what you're doing!'' Gary said angrily, his fist clenched as if ready to physically fly into Andrew.

"Just because I'm the one on the ropes with debts doesn't mean I wanted my old man dead."

"Of course you did, Gary," snapped Darlene. "You couldn't wait for him to be declared dead so you could get the insurance. And once you have it, you'll gamble it away as fast as you can."

"You're a great one to talk. Bill collectors all over the place—"

Trish got abruptly to her feet. "I've had enough of this, Lieutenant. I don't know whether Curtis told me anything about his suspicions. Whether you want to believe it or not, I don't remember any of this. When I do, believe me, you'll be the first to know!" She turned and walked out of the room. O'Donnel watched her go with a resigned expression on his round face.

Obviously things hadn't gone as well as the detective had hoped, thought Andrew. He wasn't surprised when O'Donnel stood up and gave a curt nod to everyone as he let himself out of the apartment.

Andrew had had enough of all of them, and he knew that if Curtis had said one more thing to him, he would have landed a punch on his supercilious jaw. Thinking that Trish had probably fled to her bedroom, he was surprised when he looked in the open door and saw that the room was empty. The door to the library was open but she wasn't there, either.

"She's in the sitting room," Sasha told him in the quiet voice of a conspirator when he passed her in the hall. "Is everybody gone?" the housekeeper asked anxiously in a manner that told Andrew she'd been listening to the whole fracas. He nodded, and she turned around and headed back to the kitchen.

Trish was standing in front of a window, darkened by drizzly shadows of the impending rainstorm. She looked so vulnerable, so alone that his heart caught with a tenderness that nearly overwhelmed him. She didn't turn around when he joined her at the window, and something about her remoteness kept him from putting his arm around her.

They simply stood there in silence for several minutes. Then she said in a dry voice, "That was fun, wasn't it?"

Her attempt at levity surprised him, but he answered in the same light tone, "A three-ring circus."

"Send in the clowns. There ought to be clowns," she recited in a soft whisper. Then her voice choked. "Don't bother, they're here."

Turning away from the window, she sat down stiffly on the couch, and stared at the floor.

As he eased down beside her, he asked quietly, "You okay?"

"I feel as if I'm dangerously close to falling off an edge that I can't even see."

He put his arm around her then. "I won't let you fall off."

She sighed and leaned back in the curve of his arm. A deep emotional fatigue overtook her. She was too tired to think. Too emotionally drained to feel anything. She jumped when the telephone sitting on a nearby table gave a jangled ring.

"You want me to get it?" Andrew asked.

She shook her head. A moment later, Sasha came to the door of the sitting room, and apologized for interrupting.

"It's Ms. Janelle," the housekeeper said. "She'd like to speak with you, Ms. Patricia."

Trish nodded, and took the small phone that Andrew handed her. "Yes, Janelle."

"Are you all right?" she asked anxiously. "Curtis just called the office. He's fit to be tied. He told me that O'Donnel put all of you through the third degree. I'm so sorry, Trish. Do you need me to come and be with you?"

"No, Andrew's here."

"Oh, will he be staying? I mean, I can come back over and stay the night if you're going to be alone."

Trish hesitated. All the anger she'd felt toward Andrew for not telling her about the suicide note had dissipated, and now she was embarrassed about the accusations she had thrown at him. The only time she felt her life was in any kind of balance was when she was with him. Suddenly the warm memory of their night together overshadowed everything else.

"I won't be alone." Her voice was almost a purr.

"No wonder Curtis was snarling. He said you had Andrew there looking at the computer files." Then she paused. "I want you to know that I'm not so sure Curtis's hands are clean. There have been times when I wondered if he wasn't too willing to service some of our big accounts. I mean, nobody looks for extra work unless there's a payoff."

Trish stiffened. "Curtis insisted that he told me that he suspected Perry of skimming off some of the accounts."

"The best defense is an offense, haven't you heard that? Well, anyway, don't rely on what Curtis says about anything. It's obvious he's being eaten up by a green monster at the moment. I'm glad you've got Andrew to be your protective knight."

"So am I. I think we're going back to the cottage for the night," she said impulsively.

Janelle chuckled, "Why am I not surprised?"

After Trish hung up the phone, she turned to Andrew. "Curtis called the office an told Janelle what O'Donnel had to say about the accounts. She's thinking that it might not be Perry whose been doing the skimming, but Curtis."

"That wouldn't surprise me," Andrew said, knowing full well that he was far from being unbiased in his opinion.

"I'm sorry I blew my lid this morning," Trish apologized. "You did what you thought best. Will you forgive me?"

"Always, and forever. What do you say we head for the cottage before the weather gets any worse?" An ocean breeze blowing through open doors and windows had cleared the house from any gas odor.

"All right. Do you know where this Anchor Marina is?"

"It's on the coast, a few miles after you cross the state line into New Jersey. Why? Does the name seem familiar?"

"No, but I'd like to stop there on our way to the cottage. If I was on Perry's new boat, we must have left from that marina. Maybe I'll remember something if I see it again."

THE DRIZZLING RAIN HAD thickened as they left the city. Dark clouds scudded across an overcast sky, and the car radio warned of an approaching storm whipping up the coast from Florida.

"Maybe we should put off going to the marina until tomorrow," Andrew suggested, glancing at her intense expression. Obviously, she was forcing herself to take this step even as she instinctively recoiled from it. He respected her strength of will, but he was worried that she might fall apart on him under the tremendous strain.

"No, let's do it today."

Leaving the turnpike, they drove a few miles on a side road to Anchor Marina, which was located on a small inlet with easy Atlantic access. Boats of all sizes filled the docks, and as Andrew pulled into the parking lot, Trish searched for some flickering of recognition that she'd been here before.

She studied the line of buildings edging the wharf. O'Donnel said that the white cruiser was new. *Had she come here with Perry to see his new boat? Why would they have gone out in weather like this?*

Andrew watched a deep frown settle on her forehead. Her hands were clasped so tightly that her fingernails must be biting into her flesh. He waited until she shook her head and gave him a hopeless look. "I don't remember ever being here."

"Okay, maybe we should find someone who can answer some questions."

"You can bet the police have already done that."

"Undoubtedly, but something may make more sense to you than anyone else."

"All right," she agreed, but her tone was less than hopeful as they got out of the car and headed toward a boathouse located at the entrance to the marina. The entered the small building that smelled of wet hemp and fishing gear.

A short little man with weathered skin, sandy hair and a cocky tilt to his baseball cap nodded his head in answer to Andrew's question.

"Yep, I was working that day. I told the police everything I know—which is nothing." He squinted at them. "It ain't my job to try and keep some fool from taking his boat out when there's a storm warning posted.''

Trish tried to keep her voice even. ''Do you remember ever seeing me before?''

''Nope. Just like I told the cops when they showed me your picture. I don't keep track of the comings and goings of anybody. Sure, I recognized Mr. Reynolds's picture, but I didn't pay no attention to him that day. Beats me if he was alone when the boat went out.''

''And you didn't report the cruiser missing when it didn't come back?'' Andrew asked.

''Hell's bells, how'd I know he didn't decide to put in somewhere else, or take a run down the coast? Ain't my business to keep track of these would-be Sunday sailors.''

Trish turned away without saying anything more, and walked over to the large window overlooking the marina. Storm clouds hung low and a mist floated over the water, creating a water-colored scene of rocking tethered boats. Winds whipped rain against the windowpane and made a high-pitched sound in the rafters. Vague images flashed in her mind's eye but were gone too quickly for her to grasp them. She just might be imagining them, and she shivered as a sudden chill went bone deep.

Andrew saw her trembling, and moved quickly to her side. *Had she remembered something?* His sudden hope was short-lived.

She turned to him with glazed eyes. ''I sense that there's something bubbling close to the surface, but I can't draw it out. Maybe it's just wishful thinking. If I've been here before, I don't remember it.''

''That's all right, sweetheart,'' he assured her, smiling to hide his own disappointment. ''It was worth a try. Come on, we'd better get out of here before the storm hits.''

As they hurried back to the car, a sudden spear of lightning cut across the sky, followed by vibrating thunder. Andrew kept the windshield wipers going madly as they drove along the beach road. The ocean was a churning mass of angry waves slashing the coastline with a pounding roar.

Andrew kept glancing at Trish. She sat stiffly in her seat, her color a pasty white and the muscles in her face rigid with tension.

''You okay?'' he asked anxiously.

She started to answer but the words froze in her throat as suddenly the movement of the car changed into the sensation of a whirling boat, and her whole body was caught up in a terrifying memory.

She cried out and covered her ears as slashing winds and the tumultuous roar of a pounding surge built to an excruciating crescendo in her head.

''No, no,'' she screamed.

Andrew pulled the car off the road and braked to a sudden stop. When he tried to take her in his arms, she lashed out at him with the fury of a trapped animal.

''Stop it, Trish. It's me. It's Andrew.''

She stared at him with glazed eyes and then with a whimper, collapsed against his chest. The images in her mind whirled like a runaway film, superimposing one upon the other.

''What is it, Trish? What's happening to you?''

Her voice was strained, and he bent his head close to hers. She struggled to describe the upheaval that was going through her mind and body. Every word she drew for him presented an unbelievable horror that he could picture very vividly.

Lying on the deck of a boat, she was drenched by the onslaught of sucking waves. Even as she struggled to get to her feet, she was lifted up and swept out of the boat. Somehow, she stayed afloat in the churning water, and was carried in by the surf to the beach where Andrew found her.

"Who was on the boat with you?" he prodded when she fell into silence.

"There was someone but I don't know who." Her mind was suddenly filled with ephemeral images that came and went too fast for her to hold on to them.

"Do you remember what happened before you found yourself on deck?"

She bit her lower lip so hard that her teeth left a mark. As fervently as she willed herself to remember, there was nothing recognizable that she could draw forth from the churning turmoil in her mind. Sobbing, she shook her head.

"It's okay, darling," he said, holding her close, and stroking her hair. "Don't you see? This is a breakthrough. I bet that bits and pieces of your memory will begin to surface now. We just have to be patient."

His words were intended to be reassuring but they brought their own terror. How could she continue to go through this mental torture?

Andrew waited until the tremors in her body had lessened and the fear in her anguished expression had eased before started the car again. Trish cowered against him, keeping her eyes shut and her head lowered during the rest of the drive.

They were only a few miles from the cottage, but the rain had turned into a deluge by the time they reached it, and they raced from the car into the shelter of the house. Trish dropped wearily down on the couch while Andrew quickly laid a fire in the fireplace.

"I'll get us something warm to drink," he said and started toward the kitchen just as a glare of headlights flashed across the windows. "Who can that be?"

Trish instantly stiffened. The police? Had O'Donnel come for her? Her mouth went dry and for a moment, she fought a panicked impulse to flee out the back door. The detective already had enough circumstantial evidence to charge her with murder.

As Andrew crossed the room to open the door, she stood up, suddenly too weary to fight against the inevitable.

"Come in," Andrew said, in surprise.

A wash of relief flowed through Trish when she saw that it wasn't O'Donnel in the doorway, but a split second later, a jagged memory like the piece of a jigsaw puzzled fell into place.

"No," Trish gasped, staring at Janelle. That overwhelming sense of betrayal that she'd felt before rose again in her tight chest.

As the woman stood in the doorway with the dark storm behind her, Trish's memory suddenly gave back the same picture of Janelle holding a gun, standing in the cabin's doorway, silhouetted against the slashing wind and whipping water.

"It was you," Trish croaked. "You shot Perry."

Janelle's expression tightened as a gloved hand came out of her pocket, revealing a gun. "So you remembered, Patricia. That's what I was afraid of." She motioned Andrew away from the door. "This isn't exactly the way I'd planned but the result should be the same. Two lovers found dead in each other's arms.''

''You won't get away with it,'' Andrew told her flatly, his brown eyes hard as rock.

''I wish things could be different, I really do.'' She gave Trish a tight smile. ''Even though it looked as if you were nicely in a net to take the blame for Perry's death, I knew sooner or later something would trigger your memory.''

''That's why you stayed so close to me, pretending to be taking care of me,'' Trish said in a voice that shook with a sense of betrayal. ''Why would you do it? Why would you shoot Perry?''

Janelle's mouth twisted in an ugly line. ''The two most common motives for murder, of course. Money and love. Perry and I had an affair while his first wife was alive. When she died, I expected that Perry and I would get married. Instead, he dropped me when he met Darlene, and I decided to take my revenge out in a way that would line my own nest. Unfortunately he began to get suspicions that someone was skimming money from some of the accounts, and I knew his investigation was centering on me. I heard him on the telephone setting up the date to talk to you about it while you took a spin on his new boat.''

''And you followed her there,'' Andrew said, hoping to take Janelle's attention away from Trish. He had backed up so he was standing at one end of the fireplace, and he didn't know how long she would talk before carrying out her plan to shoot both of them. His mind was racing with the urgency to take the gun from her.

Janelle glared at him. ''I had no choice. The two of

them were already talking about me in the cabin when I got there. I had to protect myself.''

As a curtain in her mind rose like the opening of a stage play, Trish said, ''You shot Perry, and I knocked the gun from your hand. We struggled and I managed to get away. I fled up to the deck but you caught up with me and hit me on the head.''

''I should have shot you then, but someone was coming out of the boathouse and I was afraid they'd see me or hear the shot. I threw off the bowline so the cruiser would drift away from its mooring. As the fierce waves quickly took the boat out to sea, I hoped that it would capsize and that would be the end of all of it.''

''Then you never really liked me, did you?''

Janelle gave a short laugh. ''It was easy to feed you stuff about shopping trips and pretend I knew all about your love life. It was laughable how gullible you were. Having O'Donnel zero in on you as Perry's killer was an unexpected benefit. Of course, I couldn't depend upon you not recovering your memory. That's why I tried to set up that suicide scam with the gas.''

''Can you really stomach killing three people in cold blood, Janelle?'' Andrew asked, as he took a step closer to her.

''Don't,'' Janelle warned, leveling the gun at him.

''Andrew, please,'' Trish cried, sensing that he would sacrifice himself to save her.

''Into the bedroom, both of you, and take off your clothes,'' Janelle ordered. ''This time there won't be any slipups.''

Andrew took a step toward Trish, then suddenly turned and hurled himself at Janelle's knees like he was making a football tackle. She went down, but as she fell, the gun went off. A deafening shot exploded in the room.

Trish felt a searing pain like a hot iron in her side. She touched a stream of warm blood bubbling up through her fingers, and her legs gave way beneath her. She slumped to the floor as a gray cloud floated her away into a blessed nothingness.

Chapter Seventeen

The same paramedics as before answered Andrew's frantic call, and Officer Baxley's patrol car was close behind. Janelle was still unconscious from the blow Andrew had landed on her jaw when she tried to get up from his tackle. He was covered with Trish's blood as he knelt beside her, trying to staunch the flow from her wound.

The ambulance took her to the little hospital where she had been before, and Andrew found himself in the same waiting room, pacing the floor and breathing prayers for her life. It was hours before she came out of surgery, but the news was good. Trish's wound was a clean one. The bullet missed any vital organs, and the doctor said that once she was moved out of the intensive care unit, her recovery should be rapid.

Andrew visited her every hour for five minutes as was allowed, but she was always asleep, and he had to be content with holding her listless hand and whispering loving encouragements.

After he watched the sun come up, he headed for the cafeteria for a cup of coffee, and was beseeched by a throng of reporters. The news media had been alerted to Janelle's confession that she had murdered

Perry Reynolds and had been foiled in her attempt to carry out a plan to make Trish and Andrew's deaths look like a suicide-murder. Flashbulbs went off in Andrew's face and a barrage of questions were fired at him. He was trying to make a retreat from the onslaught when Lieutenant O'Donnel pushed through the crowd with two other policemen, and held up his hand for silence.

"Hold it, people!" he ordered the crowd. "You'll get a news release when we have some facts to relate. Until then, clear out!" He nodded to the two policemen who moved forward and herded the protesting reporters out the front door of the hospital. Then he turned to Andrew. "Let's find someplace to sit down. You look ready to fall on your face."

When the hospital administrator stepped up and offered a small office, O'Donnel gratefully accepted. Andrew sank wearily down on a couch and put his head in his hands as the detective pulled up a chair and took out his notebook.

"I'm sorry, son, but this can't wait. We have a confession from Janelle Balfour, but I need details from you. What exactly happened?"

Andrew raised his head, and then leaned back against the couch. Staring at the ceiling, he related as best he could everything that led up to the moment when Janelle appeared at the door. He described Trish's flash of memory in the car, and her sudden remembrance when Janelle came into the house.

"So she remembers everything?" O'Donnel pressed.

"I don't know about everything," Andrew sighed. Maybe it would take a little time to recover her complete memory. And when she did, would Trish, the foundling, disappear now that the wealthy socialite, Patricia Radcliffe, had made her reappearance? Once Trish's total memory was intact, he knew that she had a business to run, obligations to fulfill, and responsibilities to pick up where she had left off.

O'Donnel asked a few more questions, and then closed his notebook. "That'll be enough for now. I'll speak to the doctor and see when I'll be able to interview Ms. Radcliffe." He paused. "Amnesia victims are a little out of my line. I missed the boat on this one," he admitted as peered at Andrew through his large glasses.

"Yes, you did," Andrew agreed shortly. He could have added that the lieutenant's handling of the case almost got Trish killed twice, but didn't.

ONCE TRISH WAS MOVED to a private room, Andrew was instantly by her bedside. "I'm here, sweetheart," he assured her when she began to stir.

Opening heavy-lidded eyes, she peered at him. Then a faint smile touched her pale lips as she said, "You look god-awful."

"Thanks," he smiled in relief. "And may I say, you've never looked lovelier."

"Liar."

He chuckled as he gently smoothed a strand of dark hair back from her forehead. "I never lie. You're beautiful and I love you."

"Tell me what happened. Janelle?"

Her worried expression convinced him that she needed to hear the truth. He assured her that the woman was in custody, and had signed a confession. "You can relax now. There's no more danger. It's all over, Trish."

"Is it?" she frowned as if trying to make all the pieces fit. "Is my memory completely back?"

"I don't know about completely. I guess that will take a little time. You may want to ease back into things slowly."

There was the hint of a sparkle in her eyes as she said thoughtfully, "Maybe I ought to go back to the cottage and spend a little time recuperating." She gave him a wan smile, closed her eyes and went back to sleep.

CURTIS PAID HER A VISIT a couple of days later, his arms filled with flowers, and deep concern etched on his face. It only took a few minutes for her to realize that any hopes she had to stay removed from the world of Patricia Radcliffe, were not going to happen. She couldn't leave the company adrift. It became apparent that her responsibilities and her commitment to the people involved in Atlantis Enterprises could not be ignored.

Curtis's relief was obvious as they began to talk about business, and he even commented that her business acumen was as sharp as ever. He also hinted at the possibility of becoming a partner now that Perry's position was open.

"I need some time to sort things out, Curtis. We'll talk later."

"Yes, of course. In the meantime, I'll make sure that everything runs as smoothly as possible. There's a woman in the accounting department that can assume Janelle's responsibilities for the time being. Her name is Sarah Henderson. She's very quick, intelligent, and she has the company's best interest at heart. I think she'd really handle the job beautifully."

Trish smiled secretly as she listened to him extol the virtues of Sarah Henderson. There was a hint of something in his voice that had to do with more than just business. She was grateful that he said nothing about resuming their old relationship, and a heavy burden was lifted off her shoulders. She couldn't help but wonder if Curtis's declared love for her in the past was based more on his desire to assume more responsibility in the company, than any undying love for her. Obviously, he felt that, given the chance, he could easily step into Perry's shoes.

Andrew was not surprised when Trish decided that she couldn't afford the luxury of hiding out at the cottage now that the full knowledge of her responsibilities had landed on her shoulders.

It was the beginning of the end.

Even though they tried to hold on to the passionate feelings that remained between them, Trish's former lifestyle began to intrude, and as the weeks passed, the distance between them widened.

They met for lunch as often as Trish's schedule would allow. When she could delay weekend meetings and conferences, they spent brief romantic trysts at the cottage. Andrew tried to be a willing escort to social affairs that demanded her appearance, but he came away feeling more like excess baggage than anything else.

He had finished his software program, and was floundering in trying to decide which new project he wanted to tackle. He turned a deaf ear to his boss's suggestion that he customize the program he'd just completed for one of their business markets overseas.

"We need someone to spend a little time in Switzerland, implementing your program toward their specific office demands. How about it?'' he asked.

''I write them,'' Andrew had replied shortly. ''Let someone else customize them.''

He struggled to concentrate on his work, and failed. The contented solitary life he'd enjoyed before a devastating mermaid washed up on his beach was gone forever. As he wrestled with his own future, the idea of getting away for a little while became more appealing. He reconsidered the offer his boss had made about sending him overseas to customize the program he had developed. Spending time in different surroundings might help soften the inevitable parting with Trish. When he mentioned it to her, he could tell that she was shaken by the sudden possibility that he would go abroad for an indefinite time.

She stared at him as if he'd suddenly become a stranger before her eyes. ''Switzerland? You're thinking of going to Switzerland?''

''Maybe it would be best—for both of us.''

She'd been finishing up some work at her desk, while Andrew sat on the white couch waiting for her. They had already been delayed going to lunch by telephone calls and last minute interruptions. ''Do you want to go?''

''You're settled in nicely now,'' he said evenly. ''Your memory is back almost a hundred percent. Your busy life is spinning off in so many directions, you won't even know I'm gone.''

''How can you say that?'' Her whole world suddenly seemed to tilt. *Andrew was leaving her.* She hurriedly sat down on the couch beside him. ''You can't go.''

His eyes narrowed. ''Why not?''

"Because...because I need you."

His smile was patient and loving. "No, you don't, love. You're a strong, independent woman who is capable of running a successful company. You know it, and I know it."

"But that doesn't have to change things between us," she argued. "And I do need you, terribly."

Trish swallowed back a lump in her throat. Didn't Andrew realize how much she depended on his quiet strength and love to help her make momentous business decisions that could make or break the company her father had left her? She had been programmed from youth to this lifestyle, and he just needed time to adjust to it. She argued that their love was strong enough to survive the challenges they faced, but when he bent his head and lightly kissed her, she knew that she had lost.

"I can't do it, live as a reflector of someone else. You've found your life, Trish, and I'm happy for you, but now I have to find mine."

"And we can't do that together?"

He remained silent and let her answer the question for herself.

THEY SAW LITTLE OF EACH OTHER in the three weeks prior to his departure. Trish's schedule was tighter than ever with board meetings and numerous business demands. They talked to each other on the phone, but Andrew had the feeling that her mind was somewhere else. He kept telling himself that it was better that way. Her preoccupation with business made it easier for him to leave.

When she showed up at the cottage just a few days before he was scheduled to leave, she looked like someone who needed some down time, and he suggested a walk on the beach to help her relax.

Slipping her arm through his as they walked, she confessed, "I feel as if I've been running to catch a bus that's already left. Not a bus, exactly, more like a plane." She tossed her head and laughed. "Yes, definitely a plane."

He searched her face and saw that her ocean-blue eyes were sparkling with suppressed excitement. "What are you trying to tell me?"

"You're not the only one who can make changes in their life."

He stopped and turned her toward him. "All right, you've got my attention."

The quickening of his breath was evident in the sudden rapid movement of his chest as she looked up into his face and said, "I've made Curtis the CEO, and decided to let him run Atlantis for me."

"But the company has been your whole life, Trish." He was dumbfounded. "You can't just give it away like that."

"I'm not giving it away," she corrected him with a toss of her head. "I'm putting Atlantis in better hands than mine, and freeing myself from the legacy that Patricia Radcliffe handed to me."

"Are you sure about this?"

She smiled as she leaned into him. "I've decided to follow my heart and spend some time abroad."

"And where you are planning on going?" he asked as he folded her into his arms.

"I was thinking Switzerland."

"Really?" he said in mock surprise as a geyser of joy shot through him.

She lifted her lips temptingly close to his. "To tell

the truth, I was thinking that a mountain chalet would be a lovely place for a wedding. That is, if a certain gentleman decided to ask me to marry him."

His smile was tender and intimate, and as he lowered his mouth to hers, his possessive kiss was all the answer she needed.

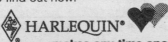

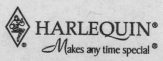

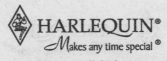